MTV's

Singled OUT

GUIDE TO DATING

ING

By Lynn Harris

Produced by
Melcher Media

Designed by
Alexander Isley Design

MTV Books/PocketBooks/Melcher Media

This book was produced by Melcher Media
170 Fifth Avenue, New York, NY, 10010

Editorial Director	Charles Melcher
Editor	Sarah Malarkey
Art Direction	Alexander Isley Design
Photography Editor	Russell Cohen
Editorial Assistant	Erin Bohensky
Photography	Adam Weiss
Illustration	Mitch O'Connell

Special Thanks to

Lisa Berger, Lynda Castillo, Gina Centrello,
Anita Chinkes, Mark Cronin, Amy Einhorn, Genevieve Field,
Lisa Hackett, Chris Hardwick, John-Ryan Hevron, Abigail Howe,
Brian Hueben, Jason Jacobs, Maureen Jay, Sheryl Jones,
Chris Kalb, Mark Kirschner, Andrea LaBate, James Massenburg,
Jenny McCarthy, Christy Nicolay, Ed Paparo,
Renée Presser, Laura Scheck, Curt Sharp, Robin Silverman,
Donald Silvey, David Terrien, Van Toffler,
Kara Welsh, and Irene Yuss.

An original publication of
MTV Books/Pocket Books/Melcher Media

Pocket Books, a division of Simon & Schuster Inc.
1230 Avenue of the Americas, New York, NY 10020

ISBN: 0671-00372-0

First MTV Books/Pocket Books/Melcher Media
printing October 1996

2 4 6 8 10 9 7 5 3 1

THE

HERS

SIDE:

Let's face it, girlfriends, we have a love-hate relationship with love.

Not love as in puppy dogs, cookie dough, and grandparents—but love as in, you know, *guys.* And they're the problem. Guys blow us off, cling too close, leave too soon, like us at all the wrong times and for all the wrong reasons. We hate them.

But we also love them. Some of them. Sometimes. There are a lot of wags and wankers, geeks and Gilligans, Barneys and bozos, whose job it is, apparently, to stand in our way and say, "I've got something in my eye . . . and it's *you!*" while all the worthwhile wonderboys slip out the back, escaping our attentions. But still, ever hopeful, we powder up and head out, thinking that maybe this time we'll snag **Mr. Right** instead of **Mr. Yeah, Right.** And sometimes, of course, we'll even go for Mr. Right *Now.* No matter what some boys may think, it's not like we are all after fused-with-Krazy-Glue commitment every time we set our sights on some unsuspecting manimal. But it is nice to find someone sweet to just kick up our heels with from time to time. All we ask is that maybe, just maybe, he will be able to operate a watch, master the art of basic conversation, and be an all-around decent dude.

With all the crowds of creeps, though, it's easy to get lost when browsing in the Guy Galleria. Where do you go for quality? What's the proper dress? How do you haggle for the best boy-bargains? Can you return faulty merchandise within thirty days?

That's what **THE SINGLED OUT GUIDE TO DATING** is all about. We'll sneak you in through the side door for a **behind-the-scam-scene** look at what men really want (not that much), what they think women want (way too much), and what **you** want (just to have some good and/or clean fun, for goodness' sake).

All right, honey, **quit dipping your toes in the kiddie pool.** Tighten your bikini and head for the deep end. It's time to swan dive into the dating pool.

Mr. Right

CHAPTER

1

When you're in the market for love, the world's your free-trade zone. It doesn't matter where you are. You could be in line at the bank, at your anthropology seminar, or in an elevator — you are always shopping.

The problem: So is everyone else. That means two things. One, you may have to engage in a tug-of-war over some hapless hunk at Neighborhood Savings, and two, you may have to fend off the unwanted advances of a nerdy

ATTENTION, SINGLED OUT SHOPPERS

CHECK OUT THE STUD SPECIALS

IN THE SUPERMARKET OF LOVE

anthropologist. There's not much you can do to avoid these pitfalls — except go in prepared.

In other words, it's best to make a list *before* you head into the Store 24 of Love. That way, while the other Bettys are wandering through the loser aisle, you're ready: You'll head straight for the highest-grade meat (or, if you're a veggie, the freshest produce).

Use this quiz to patch together your ideal boy-thing. Dare to dream a little here—it won't count toward your final grade. Later in the chapter, we'll roll up our sleeves and get real.

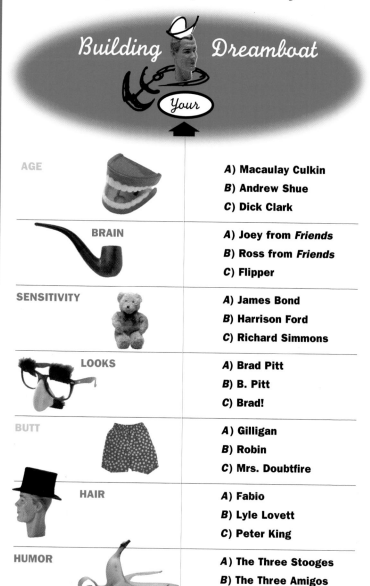

Building Your Dreamboat

AGE		A) Macaulay Culkin
		B) Andrew Shue
		C) Dick Clark
BRAIN		A) Joey from *Friends*
		B) Ross from *Friends*
		C) Flipper
SENSITIVITY		A) James Bond
		B) Harrison Ford
		C) Richard Simmons
LOOKS		A) Brad Pitt
		B) B. Pitt
		C) Brad!
BUTT		A) Gilligan
		B) Robin
		C) Mrs. Doubtfire
HAIR		A) Fabio
		B) Lyle Lovett
		C) Peter King
HUMOR		A) The Three Stooges
		B) The Three Amigos
		C) The Three Tenors
TEN YEAR PLAN		A) Mr. Mom
		B) Mr. Rogers
		C) Mr. T
CHEST HAIR		A) Fuzz-free
		B) Peach fuzz
		C) Fuzzy navel

Okay, great. You have taken the time to design the man of your dreams. Now you are prepared to spray on a little perfume, meet that perfect mate, and live happily ever after (or at least until next weekend). As if.

FROM IDEAL TO REAL
SETTING YOUR SIGHTS
WITHOUT LOWERING YOUR STANDARDS

"I was kind of disappointed by his height when I turned around and saw him. But it's not like I expected him to be the man of my dreams, anyway." —Jill, 21

So you've fantasized a bit about your dreamboat. **Now it's time to pop some Dramamine and get real.** The fact is, people who hold out for sheer perfection might just wind up in a convent. Before you take a vow of celibacy, maybe you should relax those standards a wee bit. Not that you should settle for *less*, or anything, but you might miss a real sweetie pie in your mad quest for **Mr. Perfect.** On the other hand, perhaps there have been times when you wished you were wearing a habit and singing "Kumbaya" instead of waking up next to Steve Urkel (hey, five hours and a few keg runs earlier, that man was Denzel Washington). **But don't worry.** For the most part, you'll be able to decipher just what kind of man you've attracted by paying attention and looking for the **right clues.**

> **"Looks are important, but it's really a guy's personality that makes him more—or less—attractive."** — *Lisa, 21*

At least to begin with, you have to go with the superficial and judge your prospective Romeo by what category he fits into on the grand guy-meter. Some types overlap a tad on the stud spectrum, so keep a sharp eye out when you are scoping. Sometimes — at first glance, anyway — there's a fine line between Prince Charming and the Prince of Darkness.

Handy Guy Guide

BOARD BOY
UNIFORM: Army pants cutoffs, board. Surfing and/or skating are his primary means of transportation.
PRO: Good balance.
CON: When you ask, "So, what did you today?" he responds, "Nuch. Totally scrutted grunts and I was like so beached I fully Maytagged on a monster macker. I mean, way prosecuted. But I gelled because it was totally burly out anyway and Big Mama was full of dismos and quimbys. Plus, some taste butter invited me to a skegging party. Latronic."

BAND BOY
UNIFORM: Army pants cutoffs, drumsticks in pocket. Board Boy's tuneful cousin. Can be cool, if you can drag him out of his garage rehearsal. As with Neil and Mohammed from *The Real World*, the music comes first.
PRO: Very cool to be dating "the guy in the band."
CON: Unless the band sucks.

SLACKER

UNIFORM: Black. **MOOD:** Bleak. Spends all day in café "thinking." No time for bourgeois job at Blockbuster. He's the guy with the dog-eared French-English dictionary, funny glasses, unfiltered cigarettes, and double espresso.

PRO: Can help you with your French homework.

CON: Uses French words in everyday English conversation. "Did you catch the dénouement of last night's *Melrose*? I missed it. Merde!"

SLUG

UNIFORM: By Hanes. May come out for the odd party when there's nothing good on television. No time or energy for job at Blockbuster or anywhere else.

PRO: Cable.

CON: You'll wind up paying his bill.

SENSITIVE NEW AGE GUY (SNAG)

UNIFORM: Homemade sandals, soft alpaca sweater with Inca design. Shares way too hard. Says things like, "But enough about my feelings. What are your feelings about me?"

PRO: Will gladly accompany you to chick flicks.

CON: Wants to engage in postfilm discussion to help him "understand your oppression." Be suspicious — "sensitivity" could be this week's chick-getting strategy.

VANILLA NICE

UNIFORM: Well, no one remembers what he looks like, but he has a one-syllable name. Might be *Jeff*. Sincere, caring, sympathetic, and totally, completely, mind-numbingly *blah*. Hate to dis him, but you've got to, or you'll risk an evening of nap jerks.

PRO: He really cares.

CON: You really don't.

NEWTLET

UNIFORM: Navy-blue blazer, khaki pants. Trench coat and briefcase were surgically attached at puberty. Talks earnestly about his experience at Boys State, calls your dates "meetings."

PRO: Firm handshake.

CON: Worries that French-kissing will jeopardize future bid for Senate.

SLICK WILLIE

UNIFORM: Armani. Smooth as his silk tie. A different line for every occasion, a different wine for every course. Gold-chain fashion victims hopelessly strive to be him. Really does treat you like a princess, but he's probably courting in other kingdoms, too.

PRO: Can actually dance.

CON: Tangos with ten cuties at a time.

BEAVIS

UNIFORM: Concert T-shirts from junior high. Metalhead whose innate fear of females gives him a certain scruffy charm. Drives a car with expressive muffler; still listens to the Scorpions.

PRO: Great stereo.

CON: Paying it off with his paper route.

RUDE DUDE

UNIFORM: Too dirty to tell. Beavis's bike-messenger/thrasher cousin. This Danger Boy will send a snot rocket in your direction and you'll hate yourself for laughing. Annoying, dirty, insensitive, and sometimes twistedly irresistible.

PRO: Maybe when he's not around other people he'll actually act like a decent human being.

CON: *Nah.*

JOCK OF ALL TRADES

UNIFORM: Gore-Tex. Triathlons, snowboarding, heli-skiing, you name it—this extreme sportsman may take you on some exhilarating adventures. A Dan Cortese clone with an unbelievable body, which he loves even more than you do.

PRO: Balanced diet.

CON: Can calculate his body-fat percentage on a moment's notice.

DOUBLE CON: Yours, too.

MOCK JOCK

UNIFORM: "Number One" glove, face paint. Screams things like, "You da man!" and "Yo, Ref!" Talks only about sports and only at high volume and with lots of gesticulating. Though he never made it off the bench himself, he claims to be better qualified to coach any professional sports team than its current staff.

PRO: Season tickets.

CON: You don't want to be seen with him.

JUGHEAD

UNIFORM: Glasses, backpack, Dungeons & Dragons dice. Smart *and* geeky. This guy doesn't get out in the sun much, but he could build you a solar car. Has few girlfriends he can't download. Shy and awkward, but not necessarily unappealing. At least you know there's no front—it's just him and his hard drive.

PRO: Impresses your roommates by programming your VCR with your microwave.

CON: "Entertains" your roommates by reciting *Monty Python* sketches verbatim (see "Meeting Her Roommates," page 74♂).

When you head out looking for action, remember this: The Clock of Desperation is ticking away.

CLOCK OF

NO DESPAIRATE

It's a tricky matter of timing — if you're too picky at first, you're liable to be digging through the **irregulars in love's bargain basement** by the end of the evening. Hold out too long for **Mel Gibson,** and you'll be left with the likes of **Mel Tormé.** Carry a torch too long for **Chris O'Donnell,** and **Chris Farley** will be over to snuff it out. **Jean Claude Van Damme, Dick Van Patten. Get the idea?** Sometimes it's worth making an impulse buy rather than putting your love on layaway.

Along the highway of matchmaking, your clothes are your billboard.

FASHION CRISIS

They can define you in a moment—for better or worse.

On one hand, your threads can get you noticed and remembered, but you don't want them to be *all* that gets noticed and remembered (you don't want him and his friends to refer to you forever as Fur Boots Girl). You've got to strike a balance between getting all dolled up — the fun part — and feeling comfortable — the important part. See, this is **one of the fundamental injustices of the universe:** We wear all this makeup and high heels and Wonderbras to look attractive to men, and then they turn around and say, **"I like girls who look . . . natural."** Also, if you look like you spent hours getting ready, they'll worry that if they go out with you, they'll have to spend hours waiting for you. So the point is, be sure to spend **hours to achieve the just-threw-this-on look.**

As thick as guys can be, we have to give them a little credit here: Ultimately, they're repulsed by girls who look calculated and uncomfortable in their chain-link hot pants, and attracted to girls who look uncalculated and comfortable with themselves. So your best bet is to pull enough stuff out of your closet and drawers to dam up a river, insist you have nothing to wear, realize you're late, and then fish your favorite standby outfit from the hamper.

That said, if your chain-link hot pants *are* your old standby, then go for it — because **it's not what you wear, it's how you feel in what you wear.** But just so you know, here's a guide to the first impressions the look that's truly "you" will make.

PAPER DOLL
DOLL
WARDROBE

PAPER DOLL 1A: KILT GIRL

SAYS: "Sure, I'm cute, but I can do some damage with this big old safety pin in my skirt. . . . "
1B: Throw on these accessories and whoa! Kilt Girl becomes Riot Grrl!
ROLE MODEL: Alicia Silverstone.

PAPER DOLL 2: LITTLE HOUSE ON THE PRARIE GIRL

SAYS: "I live in a sod house in Sleepy Eye. Come on over and jar preserves with me. But watch those paws—Pa's got a shotgun."
ROLE MODEL: Dr. Quinn, Medicine Woman.

PAPER DOLL 3: TARTY PARTY GIRL
SAYS: "I'm freezing."
ROLE MODEL: Kelly Bundy.

PAPER DOLL 4: BEATCHICK
SAYS: "I may rumble at poetry slams, but don't be scared away by all my existential angst. There's a shy little marshmallow floating in this quadruple latte."
ROLE MODEL: Lisa Loeb.

PAPER DOLL 5: WENT-OUT-RIGHT-AFTER-WORK GIRL
SAYS: "Pinstripes turn me on. Give me a reason to call in sick."
ROLE MODEL: Murphy Brown.

FOLLOWING YOUR MAN MAP TO DATING TREASURES

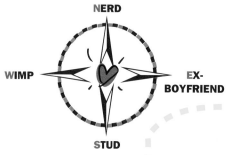

> "Clubs are kind of scary. The guys there give you these cheesy looks. They get all sweaty and do the 'schnuggle' bit. I'm like, 'Excuse me, I'm looking for my ride home.'" —*Holly, 18*

When you think *pickup scene*, you probably think bars and clubs. But think again. **Statistics show that most young people actually don't do the bar thing for dates.** They say friends, school, and parties are where the best action is. After all, anyone off the street can walk into Wham-Bam-Thank-You-Ma'am's, while the other, more specialized venues have built-in screening processes that make those critical first cuts for you. Use this map to plot your course to the place where your future honey is most likely to hang.

LEGEND

 GUY GOLD MINE

 NOT A WASTE OF TIME

 LAST RESORT (But remember: Cupid works in strange ways. Don't rule it out.)

THE VET

Odds are that **a guy with a Fluffy or Fido has room in his life**—and his apartment—for more than himself. **EXCEPTION:** If Fluffy is a python, piranha, or pit bull.

GRIZZLY ADAMS' WILDERNESS OUTFITTERS

Hang out here if you're **looking to scale Mount Datemore with a real rugged individual.** Meet him on his level with some sort of open-ended, thoughtful question, like, "Do you think mountain biking is an exciting, healthy way to experience the great outdoors? Or is it a selfish thrill sport that threatens to destroy our precious wilderness?" But remember, some of these lone wolves pack only enough trail mix for one.

END ZONE SPORTS BAR

Mock Jock Central (see page 15♀). Know the difference between illegal chucking and a double touch and you just might draw a few eyes away from the game . . . if you dare.

MONSTER TRUCK SHOW

If you're desperate enough to go this route, at least stay away from the *Playboy* Centerfold booth. But be creative: There are people there who didn't actually pay for a ticket — and you might be able to bond with them over how heinous the scene is. **Try chatting up a cop, a news photographer, or an ambulance guy waiting for casualties.** Oh, and be prepared to explain why you're there ("Uh, I'm doing a project for sociology class").

FRATERNITY ROW AT STATE U.

QUANTITY: Definitely. Houseful after houseful of **guys with backward baseball caps, enormous untied high-tops, flattops, and flat beer, all jamming to Hootie.**

QUALITY: On the other hand, can be pretty spotty. You might find yourself in a situation where the only topical opening line available is, "I never thought *Power Rangers* sheets could make such a dashing toga." Basically, pledge girl, you need to know the difference between Kappa Cool and Stigma Chi.

GROCERYLAND

No question, a tried-and-true stud emporium. But you do have to know where to look. Steer your cart first toward the organic whole foods, free-range chicken, etc.

Any guy there takes good care of himself, not to mention his Mother (yep, as in Earth). But if *you're* the one with the mother complex, head for the sugar cereal—there's probably someone there who needs help balancing his diet. (And if you really like 'em young at heart, you could always try crashing the bag boy staff meeting.)

THE MALL

The mall is a mixed bag. For high-end merchandise, **take the escalator to designer-boutique row** (a major Slick Willie haunt—see page 14♀).

The food court, on the other hand, should be used only as a place to fuel up on fro yo, *solo*. **You don't want to get mixed up with the likes of the Jamie Walters Fan Club.** As far as meeting men goes, that scene's strictly one-heart — it's the off-campus cafeteria for the headgear set.

CLEAN AND JERK'S GYM

Some clever girls take aerobics in the hopes of being scoped by the guys who loiter outside the class for that very purpose. But why waste time huffing and puffing? Go straight to the source! **Skip the class and hang with that gang of Lycra-crazed lust puppets.**

POSSIBLE APPROACH: "They sure are flexible—but so am I. Wanna spot me sometime this weekend?"

BASEBALL DIAMOND AT LONELYHEARTS PARK

Find out the schedule for the lawyers' league amateur softball world series. Then go for "a jog."

YE OLDE SOFTWARE SHOPPE

Boys and their toys. **It's the '90s version of the hardware store.** They'll say they're coming in to look for a personal finance management program, but you'll probably find them playing huge-screen interactive Doom VII (but do watch out for the eggheads).

LAST-DITCH PEP TALK

"Try to act natural, as if they were a person of the same sex. That way you can relate to them better—like they are human." — *Erika, 22*

Now that you've **worked through your quiz, thought through your timing, turned your closet inside out, and mapped your route,** just don't think about the fact that the last time you met a really cute guy was a totally random occurrence on a rainy afternoon in the library when you were sporting ripped sweats from middle school and Fiddle Faddle in your hair. Of course, these things tend to happen when you least expect them.

That said, we're not about to recommend some kind of **reverse-psychology dating strategy** that requires going without a shower and hanging out in the reference section. How much fun is that? **Half the fun is the anticipation, no matter what happens afterward.** True, after all the effort you put in, some nights you're a total loser-magnet. On others, you sit there wishing that just one loser would approach you, so that you'd at least have somebody to say no to. And yes, sometimes Mercury does align with Mars, and Adonis shows up to buy you a drink. So while you may not land a date every night, it's always worth just getting out there. **Besides, even a hellish night guarantees some killer war stories.**

So what are you waiting for? Hit the showers!

CHAPTER

2

GO GET' EM, GIRLS'!

If you can find a date at the vet or the orthodontist, more power to ya— and if you work at it, you just might. But if doing extensive fieldwork and inventing extra errands is not how you want to spend your Saturdays, there's always the old standby:

The party.

Less sleazy than Ladies' Night at the Boom Boom Room, but a tad racier than a bake sale at Our Lady of Lonely Hearts, a good party can really narrow your search for Mr. Guy.

And even a lousy party has possibilities—you just might hook up with the handsome character standing in the corner who says to you, in a husky Dylan McKay mumble, "This party's beat. Let's jump into my convertible and head out to the beach to watch the sunrise." The fact is, parties are the megamall of dating—total man-o-rama. And not only that: At a party, you've got the instant, constant, on-site feedback and backup from your most important allies in the dating wars—your friends. Read on to learn how to maximize your party potential.

WORKING THE ROOM

When you walk into a party or club, you step into an intricate web of politics, power, and deception. Things are happening all around you: alliances formed and broken, borders redrawn, downfalls plotted. **The air is thick with mousse and intrigue. "Oh, that's Julie's ex-boyfriend's cousin's best friend's soccer teammate,"** one guest whispers to another, consulting a hefty mental dossier. **"He just broke up with someone,"** she says, raising an eyebrow significantly. Seconds later, she answers another question — from someone she's not sure she can trust. **"The soccer guy? Oh, I think he's taken."**

You, of course, are right there in the inner circle. Among the familiar faces, you know exactly **who's zoomin' whom** and **who the agents of doom are.** But there are always unfamiliar players and recent developments on which your advance team must brief you promptly (more on that later). So first the obligatory hellos, then the necessary updates. And using that data, you need to make a precise and diplomatic plan. You need to protect your own carefully formed allegiances (i.e., **do not dis your sistahs**), but you also need to look out for numero uno (**your sistahs will understand**) — and you've got to have eyes in the back of your head. The moment you turn to not look like you're checking your hair in the TV screen, an enemy operative could move in on Julie's ex-boyfriend's cousin's best friend's soccer teammate.

Here are the blueprints: Now go stake out your territory.

1. FOOD TABLES/BAR

Need for swift traffic flow in this area provides opportunity both for initial eye contact and speedy escape.

2. BATHROOM/LINE FOR BATHROOM

Rendezvous point, where you can gather six at a time for emergency meetings. Synchronize your watches. When one of you doesn't show up, you'll know she's hooking up.

3. COUCH/SEATING AREA

Go in only if you have a plan for getting out.
THE RISK: Those soft cushions can suck you in and down, leaving you wedged between a sharp elbow and a dull boy.

4. STEREO/BAND

Two potential uses: **(1)** scoping the bass player; **(2)** escaping from boring conversationalist by relocating to speaker area— too loud to keep talking!

5. DANCE FLOOR

PRO: Good place to make yourself available.
CON: May require actually dancing with guy (see "Legion of Dancing Doom" page 29 ♂).

6. KITCHEN

Avoid. Unflattering light.

7. POOL TABLE

Steer clear, unless you fall into one of two categories:
(1) tough girl who can kick the guys' butts (which guys love/fear); or **(2)** helpless giggling girl who says, "Oooh, can you show me how to hold the big stick and hit the little ball?" Otherwise you should spare yourself the agony.

The whole point of dating is, well, to date. But honestly, dating would be practically pointless if it weren't for your friends. You know, you get ready together, you work the room together, you blow each other off for the guys you meet, and then you get together for frappuccino the next day to compare notes. Your friends are both your conscience ("You really shouldn't rekindle things with Jay . . .") and that little devil guy on your shoulder (" . . . because his *friend* looks like a total fox").

They are there to pick you up when you get rejected, to help you let the guy know he's scum, and if necessary, to go out with him themselves.

The **support that** gal pals **provide** in the world of dating is not only emotional but also tactical. You and the girls can serve many purposes for one another when you're on the front lines:

Hanging with the Girl Gang

THE POSSE

Men go courageously into war, take over multinational corporations, slay dragons, do karaoke. But the mere sight of a group of women is enough to send those big brave bruisers crawling under the covers with a flashlight and a stuffed bunny. A group of women is men's second worst nightmare (the first: being laughed at by a group of women). Leave one boy stranded among three or more girls and paranoia takes hold. "What are they talking about?" "How much do they know about me?" "She's twisting her earring—is that girl code for 'I'd date him . . . on a bet'?" (For more paranoid male misinterpretation, see "Watching the Signs," page 32 ♂.)

Enjoy this power while you can. But keep in mind that it also means that at some point you probably need to split up, maybe work the room in pairs.

THE ELECTRIC EYE

Women have three bionic senses: **(1)** the ability to distinguish between jade and teal; **(2)** ultrasonic hearing that makes our ears painfully sensitive to nonringing phones; and **(3)** eyes in the backs of our heads (which work well even when we're wearing a cute hat).♀

♀ Unfortunately, however, the X-ray vision that would allow women to detect the shriveled heart of a jerk through the fleecy sweatshirt of a nice guy does not seem to have fully evolved.

It is this last ability that will serve you best under dating circumstances. At a party, bar, or other scene, **your girl gang will see and know all:** who's available, who's taken, who's soon to be taken, who's checking whom out, who's coming closer, and who's to be avoided at all costs. **And knowledge means power.**

THE ONLY DRAWBACK: Knowledge also means no surprises. And surprises are fun, whether they're nice or nasty. Let's say that your friends don't warn you that Oily Boy is on the prowl. There's no time to escape — he taps you on the shoulder, startling you and causing you to shower your rum punch all over Señor Hot Prospect, whom you've been buttering up all evening. Hottie takes off; now you're stuck with Oily. Not the ideal outcome, to be sure, but still good for hilarious groaners with the girls later.

So once again, at some point it may be wise to split up.

THE FORCE FIELD/THE DECOY

When you hang with the homegirls, you can protect each other by **using your special gal powers** to shield your compadres from undesirable greasers or to alert them to the approach of munchable menfolk. When necessary, assume strategic positions and switch the force field on with the following command:

> "Omigod-he's-right-over-there-quick-get between-me-and-the-bar-and-walk-right next-to-me-to-the-bathroom."

Likewise, the decoy is activated by:

> "Omigod-I-think-he's-coming-over-please talk to me-talk to me-talk to me."

Both systems are invaluable.

So even if you split up, at least continue to travel in twos.

I SAW THE SIGN:
KNOWING WHEN TO MAKE YOUR MOVE

Things were much more clearly defined back when you could simply **bat your lashes** or **drop a perfumed hanky.** Try one of those tricks nowadays and a guy's likely to think you've got something stuck in your eye, or worse, your nose. The good news, though, is that now a gal can skip the props and go right up and talk to a guy. In fact, guys love it.

But maybe they love it too much. When you start the small talk, you're just doing a preliminary check . . . and he's already wondering if you're on the Pill. You've got to find a safe middle ground between the risk of rejection (unlikely though it may be) and the risk of making Mr. Gigolo think you're hotter for him than you really are. Before you make your move, watch for signs and read them carefully. Subtle, hard-to-get flirtation on his part is a green light for you, but the harder his sell, the more wary you should be. Use this handy chart as your guide.

"I Saw the Sign" Signal Scenarios

SIGN	GREEN
He makes eye contact.	He looks at you, looks away, looks back.
He and his friends move en masse to a closer table.	But proceed to ignore you.
He maneuvers closer to you at bar.	But he proceeds to ignore you entirely.
He steps toward dance floor.	And appears to discern presence of beat.
He seems to be waiting for you outside.	And looks up at you shyly when you exit.

WATCH
YOUR STEP: TOP 5 SIGNS THAT HE'S TAKEN.

1. STROLLER

2. RING

3. RING TAN-LINE

4. HICKEY

5. ID BRACELET THAT SAYS "ASHLEIGH"

YELLOW	RED
He raises one eyebrow.	He raises both eyebrows and wiggles them Groucho Marx–style.
And then he raises his glass to you in a toasting motion while friends grunt approvingly.	And then he smashes glass against the wall, shouting, "Damn it all, woman, I want you!"
But he moves closer to you with his nightmare friend in tow.	And mouths the words *I love you.*
And slaps thigh in time to music.	And points at you, beckons with forefinger, then points at dance floor.
Where he drives up in his custom-painted van.	Oh, he's the valet.

CHAMPIONSHIP DON'T-COME-BACK'S

1. "The full moon turns you on? Oh, thanks, that reminds me, I've got to go comb my face."

2. "I look familiar? Oh, you must have seen me on the *America's Most Wanted* female-serial-killers special."

3. "What's a nice girl like me doing in a place like this? Not talking to you."

4. "I'm sorry, I don't speak English."

5. "Do I come here often? Do you leave alone often?"

6. "What's my sign? *This* [the bird]."

"One thing that works is to say, 'I'm just getting over a relationship.'" — *Katie*, 19

FLIRTING 101: CAN WE TALK?

"This guy comes up to me at the mall and says, 'So, am I going to see you tomorrow?' I say, 'What?' And he says, 'You know, on the cover of *Cosmo*.' I was like, 'You've got to be kidding me.'" — *Isabel*, 18

Okay, it's time to swing into the conversation portion of this pageant. Chatting isn't necessarily a big deal, but the cuter your prey, the bigger your palpitations.

What if you say something dumb? What if you hiccup? What if you laugh admiringly at one of his jokes and Coke comes out your nose?

All of this worrying is really unnecessary. First of all, guys are more scared of talking and flirting than you are. They'd almost rather be *dancing*, for God's sake. Besides, **they're not paying a bit of attention to what you're saying;** *they're watching what you're doing.*

See, guys are really superstitious. They think everything is a *sign*. Now, we're not talking about signs like, say, an ache in their knee means it's going to rain, or anything they can read in their tea leaves (how many guys do you know who drink tea, or who will admit that their knee hurts?).

What we are talking about is the fact that he will take everything you do now as an indication of something you might do later, if you get the picture (see "Watching the Signs," page 32 ♂).

Remember, this means that **he is not actually listening to what you're saying.** You could say, "Come home with me *now*, carry me up my ladder, take me on my loft . . . oh, and my roommate will join us after her photo shoot," and he'd be thinking, It's no good, she looked at her watch.

Men listen only for the key words they need in order to formulate their own response to your sentence (and when they are feeling particularly chatty, they may actually work in a follow-up question, as in, "You're from Pasadena? Oh, yeah, I know some people from there. Do you?"). So it really doesn't matter what you say, as long as you don't let slip any really alarming key words, such as *lice, flesh-eating virus,* or *relationship*.

Otherwise, it's all about body language. Smiles are good, as are hair flips (these days, that's unisex). Little "accidental" touches ("Oh, excuse me!") are nice, a little forward. (Bonus: "Oh, excuse me!" + hair flip.) Smiles with tongue-on-teeth are definitely racy, unless you've got something wedged up there next to your incisor.

Note: Boys do actually listen sometimes to what you're saying, especially when it's delivered in conjunction with potentially promising actions, such as, "This straw's too small for my mouth — could you grab me a few more?"

THE 411
ON PHONE NUMBERS

Is it okay for a girl to ask a guy for his number? We polled every single male in America over the age of twelve and got the following response from 125 percent of them (margin of error = 0):

"Duh!"

Honestly, it's a win-win situation. In 99 percent of cases he'll be totally flattered, not to mention relieved (the remaining 1 percent will say something like, "My, my, I'm not sure it's appropriate for a lady to be so forward," in which case, well, you'll know right then that you don't want to be making expensive phone calls *backward in time*). And if you change your mind later, you don't *have* to call him (in fact, each time you *don't* call undoes years of oppressive phone silence caused by men who have done the same).

So when in doubt, get the digits — and you can decide later whether to dial or dis.

Then, of course, there are those 911 moments when some major goober pesters you for your number. Of course, you can always make like Nancy Reagan and just say no. But you could have a little more fun if you like. How about tossing out a few nonsense digits that will send the weenie straight to operator oblivion every time he tries to call you?

1. "Oh, that's awfully sweet. But as an Amish maiden, I have no phone. Ooh, that's my buggy — I'm Audi."

2. "Jeez, I'd love to give it to you, but you should know that telephone hours at New Beginnings House are between five and six in the morning, just before we head out to spear trash on the highway. Still want it?"

3. "Oh, I don't think you want to do that" — (hastily look behind you, then lean in and whisper) — "*they're always listening.*"

4. "Gee, phones are okay, I guess. But a gal misses the old-fashioned and dying art of letter writing. What do you say I give you my P.O. box instead?"

5. "Terrific! And while I'm at it, let me give you my fax, portable fax, car fax, cell phone, car phone, e-mail address, backup e-mail address, beeper, sky page. And also my Web site. So when can I expect to hear from you?" (See "Madam President," page 15 ♂).

THE
DATE

"You gotta talk on the phone first before you go out. Otherwise you'll be out with someone and he'll say, 'Oh, in my spare time I worship Satan and shovel garbage.' And you're in public with this guy!" —*Alexis,* 18

We asked the same sample of males over twelve whether it was okay for a girl to call a guy once she had his number, and funny, their answer was also

"Duh!"

But you still may have a case of the willies (which should give you some sense of what guys have gone through since the invention of the telephone). And why is that? First, there's Fear of Rejection, which, as you now know, grows like a fungus on all phone lines, no matter what the caller's gender. But more specifically, when women call, the ante is upped. On one hand, we hear over and over that guys are flattered when girls call. But we also have evidence that they are *frightened,* as if they envision you modeling your wedding dress in the three-way full-length mirror on your end on the portable phone.

Truth is, as far as you're concerned, this first phone call is merely an interview request, a follow-up to the first meeting (the cover letter). How should you express your interest and maintain his... without letting him think you're calling to offer him a lifetime position in the family firm?

The Calling Calendar

FRIDAY — Day You Meet!

SATURDAY — Too Soon Psycho Alert!

MONDAY — Still No! a bit needy

TUESDAY — Earliest Possible Call: but you've really left him no time to wonder

WEDNESDAY — Keep letting him sweat it if you can!

THURSDAY — Call for Weekend Plans!

WEEKEND — Don't call if you haven't already: let him think you have a life.

NEXT WEEK — Fair Game!

WEEK AFTER — Fair Game: but lie & say you've been out of town.

Detective Work

You've got the conversation-ball rolling, and you're pretty sure you're going to ask him out—but first you should do a subtle background check. Ask a few innocent-sounding questions that may shed some light, such as:

TO FIND OUT:	YOU ASK:
IF HE LIVES AT HOME	"Oh my God, I have the landlord from hell. What's yours like?"
IF HE HAS A CRIMINAL RECORD	"I need some parts for my Nissan — know a good chop shop?"
IF HE IS RELIABLE	"Do you happen to have the time?"
IF HE RESPECTS WOMEN	"Could you tape the NCAA women's hoops finals for me? My roommate wants to watch the Playmate Olympics on ESPN2 — and it's his TV."
IF HE HAS A GIRLFRIEND	Use the word *scrunchie* in a sentence and see if he understands you.

Date, Time, and Place

You have to do most of the work here, because boys are a little thick about plans. The watches they wear are purely ornamental (or are they? See "First Date Instruction Manual, Part One," page 54 ♂), as are the calendars they own ("Co-eds of the Big Ten"). So you need to be specific, because no matter what you ask them about, they'll say,

"Yeah, I should be free."

EXAMPLES:

NOT ENOUGH: "You want to check out the Connie Selleca retrospective sometime?"

HE'LL SAY: "Yeah, I should be free sometime."

ENOUGH: "You want to check out the Connie Selleca retrospective at the Plaza Twin Saturday afternoon?"

HE'LL SAY: "Yeah, I should be free then."

A LITTLE MUCH: "I'm naked."

HE'LL SAY: "Yeah, I should—huh?"

Setting It Up

" I want a challenge. I don't want a guy who's going to wait on me hand and foot. I can get my own glass of water. " —*Tina, 23*

If you're doing the asking, **you need to select a venue** that allows for further investigation into three important qualities: his reliability, his verbal ability, and his personal hygiene. Here's how this translates into the essential characteristics of your date locale.

HIM	DATE PLACE
RELIABLE?	Requires promptness/ reservations
VERBAL?	Requires quiet atmosphere
DOMESTICATIBLE?	Requires utensils, good lighting

In other words, you need to go to a restaurant. And a pretty good one at that—but not too intimidating. **Nothing that starts with** Mc, but, then again, **nothing that starts with** Chez either.

Now let's say he's asked you out.

The invitation itself provides many opportunities for advance information. First of all, what if he says,

"So, wanna get together sometime?"

"Sure, like how about a bus trip to Blahsville?"

Can't he do better than that?

DATE	GAB FACTOR?	SEE BE SEEN?
MOVIE AT THE MULTIPLEX	He's not a talker.	Cause for concern, unless he's taking you somewhere light afterward.
PLANET HOLLYWOOD	He's not a talker (especially when he is rendered speechless by the sight of Pamela Anderson Lee's bustier from *Barb Wire*).	He wants to show you off ... to a bunch of tourists from Idaho.
LAKERS GAME	Not so high, but better than if he'd asked you to his house to watch the game with his roommates.	Medium. He's not exactly showing you off to an intimate group of his closest friends, but he is willing to risk being seen with you on television.

Big nay. Or almost as bad,
" I'm up for anything—whatever you want to do."

This guy needs a spine transplant. In an ideal world—and let's hope this isn't too much to ask—he'll have some specifics lined up. Here's an underground guide to what goes into those choices (for a look at his invitation motivations, see "The Game Plan," page 47 ♂):

BUCKS?	HEARTS AND FLOWERS?	ACTION POTENTIAL? DO NOT DIS-TURB
Matinee of *Escape from Witch Mountain*? Not your sugar daddy (though he may spring for one).	If he's willing to sit through anything with Whoopi Goldberg, Olympia Dukakis, Maya Angelou, and Mary Something Something, this could be serious.	Fun to watch him agonize over how to make eighth-grade make-out moves (arm stretch, hand shift, etc.).
Twenty dollars for a Pauly Shore Surf 'n' Turf? He's gotta think you're worth it.	Not unless he thinks Jason's mask or Schwarzenegger's Uzi will melt your heart.	Action *figures*, maybe.
Depends on where your seats are.	Believe it or not, yes. Men don't take just any chick to the temple of testosterone. He's allowing you into the inner circle. This is up there with meeting his mother. Could be serious.	Speed, sweat, Lakers girls. He'll need *some* kind of release . . .

DATE	GAB FACTOR?	SEE BE SEEN?
HARBOR CRUISE	Plenty. He's confident enough to be trapped on the Lido Deck with you and forced to make conversation.	Promising. He wouldn't have just *anyone* on his arm at the captain's table.
LASERIUM (LIGHT SHOW, NOT TATTOO REMOVAL)	If you speak Klingon, maybe.	Yeah, if he wants to show you off to his Stanley Kaplan class.
IN-LINE SKATING	He can talk for hours about how much you suck.	A good sign. He thinks you'll look good in sunlight and/or spandex.
SMASHING PUMPKINS CONCERT	Probably not a talker — depending on how close to the amps he wants to stand.	Great. Willing to parade you around in front of a hip crowd.
EVENING AT THE IMPROV	No, or the comedians will rag on him.	Good. He knows the comedians will heckle him if he shows up with a double-bagger.
WRESTLING CHAMPIONSHIP AT PALACE O' MUD	Not a reader.	Could be worse. Could ask you to watch it on pay-per-view.

BUCKS? 	HEARTS AND FLOWERS?	ACTION POTENTIAL? DO NOT DIS-TURB
He's forking over a pretty penny for you — unless he's also the guy who swabs the decks.	Major. Might even be a little overboard in this regard (as in, there'll be a band playing "Tie a Yellow Ribbon").	Depends on size of ship, motion of ocean.
Whoopee. Maybe he'll spring for gum, too.	Your only hope is a candlelit dinner at Chuck E. Cheese afterward.	Hard to get anything going when his mother is driving you home.
Good if he's springing for rentals. Bad if he "happens" to have an "extra" pair of women's skates at home.	Could be cute — unless he's trying to unload his ex-girlfriend's skates on you.	Not until he takes a shower.
Good. Even better if he can afford to get tickets from a scalper.	A special concert in the park, maybe. But not if they are playing the Humonga Dome.	Not if he's scoping the cute bass player.
Yeah. He'll have to pay off the comedians to quit ragging on him and keep you in triple mai tais all night.	Oh, sure — you, your date, a candle, a $12 cocktail, and jokes about how much love sucks.	Only insofar as the comedians will quiz you about your sexual practices.
Could be worse. Could ask you to watch it on his frat's pay-per-view.	Could be less romantic. Could be a cockfight.	Only if you are a contestant.

So, What Are You Going to Wear?

Your first meeting was probably in some dark place, clouded by a gauzy haze of hyper hormones and stale beer. On your date, however, the lights may be brighter and his eyes may be sharper — **so what you wear will be much more important.**

SOME ITEMS TO WATCH OUT FOR

DON'T WEAR	UNLESS YOU'RE
A CUTE HAT	*really* cute (or slightly balding)
UNDERWEAR AS OUTERWEAR	the Maidenform Woman
HIP BOOTS	going fly-fishing
NOSE RING WITH CHAIN ATTACHED TO EARRING	outwitting the notorious Nose Robber
MACRAMÉ	a spider plant

SEEING YOUR WAY THROUGH THE  DATE

Most often, you're out on a proactive prowl. But sometimes, for better or for worse, there are dates that come to you. You know, the kind of date you go on as a favor to someone, or as a favor to yourself (as in to make someone stop bugging you to do it). Or, well, because you need a date. Yep, it's the old warhorse for dateless desperadoes (and desperadas): The blind date.

Here's the problem with blind dates — **you can't write them off completely.** Sure, most of the time you wind up spending the evening discussing Melvin's collection of gourds that resemble past U.S. presidents. But there's always, always that slender chance that this time, despite all the geek hell you've endured in the past, things might turn out differently. There's got to be **some blind date success story** stuck in your mind — you know, somebody's great-aunt Opal who met her husband of seventy-five years on a blind hayride or something. You think, Well, what can I lose **as long as the date takes place somewhere suitably dark,** and obscure, and far, far away from anyone who knows people who know me?

So go with it.

A CAUTIONARY NOTE

TAKE ONE MORE MOMENT TO LOOK CLOSELY AT THE TERM BLIND.

It's crucial to decipher those code words your girlfriend uses when she insists that you meet the Greek exchange student living next door to her aunt in Fresno. Here's how.

CODE WORD	MEANS
EURO	his mother's from Winnipeg
KINDA CUTE	short
NICE	flatliner
GREAT PERSONALITY	loud
GOOD SENSE OF HUMOR	really loud
HILARIOUS	really, really loud
SMART	quiet

Now, let's say, just in case, that despite all your advance information, you make a bad call. Under most circumstances, a good sailor will stick out the voyage. At least you can return to port with a story good enough to actually make a rotten date seem semiworthwhile. **But what if you make a really, really, really bad call???**

You should be prepared for the major Mayday situation that could force you to jump ship.

If the needle on your **ANNOY-O-METER** has spun off its coil, you are going to have to think fast. Remember, this guy is your mother's best friend's nephew. You can't just ditch him for no apparent reason, and being nasty will only make things worse. The trick is to concoct a plausible lie that will get you out of there with no questions asked. Here are a few keys to the escape hatch.

PLAN AHEAD No matter what, before you head out the door with mystery man, ask a friend to beep you midway through the evening. If things are going well, ignore it. But if he's serenading you with the entire score from *All Dogs Go to Heaven 3*, go to the phone, come back looking a little wigged out, and say:

"I'm sorry—I've gotta go. It's too hard to explain. Here's my share of the bill."

Normally, this would be too vague, but the beauty of this caper is that the beeper lends your lie that critical dollop of reality.

Or, after polishing off half your swordfish steak, remember that you are "allergic" to swordfish. Say something like,

"Oh, my. That was silly of me. In exactly twenty minutes I will be covered in festering, contagious hives. The best thing for me to do is grab a cab and get home to my ointment before it's too late. Here's my share of the bill."

Or, say the following: **"Wow! Who would have thought that little old me would be sitting here with the vice president of the Young Chemists of Greater Cucamonga. I'm so . . . ohmigod — the iron!"** Run like the wind and don't look back.

"Just be yourself. Never put up a front. Your true colors come out in the long run. If they don't like you for who you are, just keep on looking." — *Sabrina, 24*

If your mother were writing this book, she would tell you that all you need to do on your first date is "be yourself."

You can't say, **"Ma, how am I supposed to be myself when all he's doing is wondering what I look like with my clothes off?"** (Or, more accurately, **"Ma, how am I supposed to be myself when all I'm doing is wondering what he thinks I look like with my clothes off?"**)

We know, it's tough. But your mom does have a point. Now is not the time to try to be someone you're not. If you do, you'll wind up having to walk the talk in some hellish way later ("Clogging!? I love clogging! It's a beloved art my family brought here from the old country. Oh — be your Clog-a-Thon partner? Uh, I'd love to . . .").

The fact is, of course, that you're both still in evaluation mode. Otherwise you'd just skip the formalities, do the nasty a few times, and *then* decide if you could stand each other.

But that's just not how it works. **You have to go through all this "date" business:** It's like a little show, or a segment on the Home Shopping Network, where each of you is trying to make the item (yourself) look its best, so that the other will figure it's worth reaching for a credit card. But you don't want to do any false advertising. Someone shopping for a diamond is going to be mighty disappointed when he finds out he's got cubic zirconia on his hands. **That merchandise will go straight back to sender.**

So if you give him a pretty accurate picture on the first date and you don't turn out to float his boat, then at least you won't be left wondering, **"Okay, so no go on Farm Girl, maybe I should have gone with Jock Chick."** Nah — you'll just know that *he* is the one who's severely taste-impaired.

This brings us to the best reason of all to try to be yourself: If you're sitting there worrying about how to crook your little finger or what on earth Ms. You're Vegan? . . . Uh, Me, Too! should order, then you've got no brain cells left for the million dollar question:

Does *he* float *your* boat?

Some would say that it's all a matter of chemistry, that I-just-knew thing referred to by your older female relatives (you know, the divorced ones who are "starting over" in Boca). Yeah, well, when you evaluate Mr. Maybe, just skip the chemistry achievement and go straight for the essay questions. In general, as we've said before, you want to look for that happy middle ground: attentive but not obsessive, strong but not silent, nice but not NutraSweet. And intelligent, but definitely not smart enough to know that, throughout the date, you'll be administering:

The First Date Aptitude Test

AS THE RENDEZVOUS WEARS ON, ASK YOURSELF THE FOLLOWING QUESTIONS AND MAKE THE FOLLOWING OBSERVATIONS:

Part 1: The Arrival

PUNCTUAL	TARDY	TARDY AND CLUELESS

Is he punctual (at least no later than you)? If he's outside the ten-minute "Traffic sucked!" window, put him on probation: possibly inconsiderate, unreliable. What if you were going into labor and he had to get to the hospital, for God's sake?! Hold on, we're getting carried away. Anyway, if he's late and he doesn't apologize, double probation: Guaranteed, he's the same kind of guy who "doesn't see" junk on the floor or crumbs on the counter.

EXCEPTION: If you later find out that a teeny little fashion crisis on his part caused the delay, drop the charges. That's cute.

| COUPLE
MINS. EARLY | 20
MINS. EARLY | MORE THAN 20
MINS. EARLY |

Or is he early? How early? A few minutes: nice. More than twenty: a little creepy. Stayed overnight in a sleeping bag outside, just to make sure: scram! (unless this stunt scored you guys front-row at a Foo Fighters concert).

| SQUINT | HUG | TONGUE |

Finally, how does he greet you? If he's at all squinty, hesitant: caution—he's not sure he remembers what you look like (or, if it's because he got new contacts just for the date—well, that's overdoing it a bit). Hug: cute. Double-cheek kiss: cute, but only if he's actually European. Any tongue at all: scram! (or skip the Hard Rock and get a room).

Part 2: The Activity

| MANNERS? | WELL-MANNERED | OVERBEARING |

Let's say, for the sake of argument, that you've met at a restaurant. Basically what you're looking for is a gentleman, but not one from the days when women weren't allowed to vote or taught to read. So, for example, pulling your chair out for you is nice; saying, "The lady will have . . ." before you've looked at your menu is not.

| MUTTERER | CHATTERBOX | LOUDSPEAKER |

The meal is also a chance for a sound check.

Just like guys fear being spotted with ugly girls, girls fear being heard with loud men. He could have **headgear, high-water pants,** and a **unibrow,** and **you could deal as long as he was quiet.** So how's this guy's volume? Ideally, more than a mutter (too shy, not good with parents), but less than a walking PA system (too much, not good with humans).

Four Flirting Techniques He'll Be Looking For

These little gestures will make **Mr. Maybe very, very happy.** Do them even if you're not sure you want this thing to last any longer than one date. It's always fun to see a guy sweat.

1. SPARKLY LAUGHTER AT HIS JOKES
(definitely specify, "Ooh, you're so funny!" or he'll worry that you're laughing at him).

2. MEANINGFUL ARM TOUCH
(to be used every time you say, "Oh, my God!" or "Me, too!").

3. MEANINGFUL FOOT TOUCH
(say "sorry", but leave feet touching).

4. SPILLING YOUR WATER RIGHT DOWN THE FRONT OF YOUR WHITE T-SHIRT
(say, "Eggplant photosynthesis Barry Manilow." He won't hear a thing).

BONUS ROUND DO ALL FOUR AT ONCE.

Handy Clip 'n' Save Feature
LET'S GIVE HIM SOMETHING TO TALK ABOUT

One way to make a guy describe you as really interesting is to ask him a lot of questions that allow him to go on at length. These include:

1. DO YOU WORK OUT?

2. ARE YOU INVOLVED IN ANY SPORTING ACTIVITIES?

3. CARS: PRO OR CON?

4. WHAT IS THE DEAL WITH DENNIS RODMAN?

5. HOW DOES A HAM RADIO WORK?

6. WHAT'S YOUR POSITION ON NAFTA? (JUST WANTED TO MAKE SURE YOU WERE PAYING ATTENTION!)

SUSHI

Too big for one bite, too difficult to bite in half. You'll wind up gnawing and having it fall apart, or stuffing the whole thing in and making him wait while you chew.

OVERSTUFFED SANDWICHES

Too tall to bite into; filling will unload out the back.

VEGETARIAN RESTAURANT

Your stomach will be growling audibly within thirty minutes.

PASTA

Only in small pieces, like ziti; otherwise you'll get noodle whiplash on your face.

CHICKEN IN ANY FORM BUT BONELESS

No way to eat without looking like you were raised by wolves.

"JUST DRINKS"

Liquid dates: only if you want to find out from someone else how your date went.

NOTE: Nachos are great flirting food: lots of tongue action, finger licking, becoming flushed and undoing top button after eating whole jalapeño "by mistake."

Part 3: The Aftermath

The sun is setting, dinner is digesting, the credits are rolling... where do you go from here?

Sometimes, for better or for worse, the situation is as clear as day. You may be able to tell from how he wraps things up. As you get up to go, does he leave you with your own private ID code for his beeper, or bus fare? Does he say anything like, "Well, now that I've paid for drinks and dinner, I suppose you'll be coming back to my place?" That's when you'll know you'll be going home alone — and maybe even changing your phone number.

Otherwise, though, you are entering the **Twilight Zone of dating.**

Signals any fuzzier than the above are tough to read. If he seems to want to go right home, is that because he's a gentleman . . . or because his roommate "has the room" tonight? Hard to say. And besides, don't forget this important question: What do *you* want to do? This is the '90s, ladies:

Keep him or dump him? Or keep him — for tonight?

Keep him or dump him, but remember to play it safe when it comes to sex. As we said, this is the '90s ladies, Be sure you're packing latex!

Hate to say this, but you know what? As far as figuring out what your next step is, well, *you'll just know.*

THE WRAP-UP

"Goodnight, Fred" or *"Hello, Sailor"*?

So the night isn't as young as it used to be. It's time to think about what kind of goodbye you'd like. Will it be the "You're really nice, but . . . " goodbye or the "You have a really nice butt" goodbye?

We'll get back to kissing in a bit, but first—just in case—let's get dissing out of the way. Guys and subtlety—it's an oil-and-water kind of thing. Sometimes you have to clobber them on the head with rejection for them to take a hint. But don't come down too hard—those same big beefy Brutuses you see bench-pressing megaweights at the gym are actually delicate little flowers inside (see "How to Take A Dump" page 64 ♂).

Here are a few road-tested and reliable ways to sugarcoat a see-ya:

"We should all go out sometime."

Effective, but still nice. You are saying, "I wouldn't mind being in the same room with you again, but only if there are several other people creating a buffer between us."

"I just broke up with someone. I need some time alone before I start seeing anyone."

Works like a charm. In girl-time, of course, *just* can mean anything from "two weeks ago" to "in eighth grade."

"You're really, really great and I really, really like you . . . as a friend."

Sounds warm and fuzzy enough, but keep in mind that when you deliver the last three words, what happens in boy's-eye-view is the following: Your head spins around 360 degrees, your pupils roll back into their sockets, and you spew green bile all over his bucket seats.

Apply lipstick shortly before the moment of truth. Boys don't know what to make of that.

But if he **might be a keeper**—at least for a while — how do you let him know? It's not enough just to be nice. **Why?**

Because he'll think you're, well, just being nice. Boys are often more perceptive than we give them credit for, but not in this department (it's kind of the opposite of when all you do is ask a guy at the gym to spot you, and he thinks, She wants me!). But since he's not exactly a bloodhound, **you have to spell**

things out just enough to keep him interested — while still preserving **the thrill of the chase** for yourself.

To give him the green light, try some of the flirting techniques mentioned on page 54♀, adapted for a standing position if necessary. Another possibility: Let a couple of beats of silence pass, then look up at him slightly shyly from underneath the lock of hair that has—cross your fingers—tumbled adorably down past your eyebrow. If he doesn't take the hint and plant one—well, that's a no-brainer.

Either

(A) he doesn't like you, or (B) he does like you.

OPTION (A) seems practically too ridiculous to address. *Hello?* Why would a guy not want to kiss someone reasonably pleasant, fragrant, and *there?* But it happens. Sometimes, and most often with sucky timing, the "fact" that all guys want action all the time proves itself false.

OPTION (B) is annoying when it happens, but really, really cute if it's true. Yep, it's possible that he likes you too much to kiss you, that he's paralyzed with fear of screwing something up. How can you tell? You'll know. You can feel it. He'll look at you a little funny, promise to call, hesitate for a moment, then take off.

OPTION (C) is too unthinkable to have mentioned earlier, but here it is now: When you go inside and look in the mirror you discover that the reason he looked at you funny and hesitated was that he could find no delicate way to tell you that most of your spinach salad had adhered to your top row of teeth. We're not even going to talk about that.

THREE TYPES OF GOODNIGHT KISSES
A CLOSE READING

"A peck on the cheek means we are going to keep in touch as friends, not start a relationship." —*Sam, 24*

THE PECK

Means, "Gee, you're such a swell gal, Polly, but I just don't see us going steady on account of, well, I'm just not all that attracted to you." Or, "Gee, you're such a swell gal, Polly, that I can't see slipping you tongue until the second date."

VARIATION: THE DOUBLE PECK, which means that he's

(A) European, or **(B)** the kind of guy who went to London for two weeks last year and still uses that fake accent.

THE PLANT

Promising. A definite *kiss* kiss. Not mistakable, say, for his lips landing on your face when he trips. Says, "We'll stop short of a full make-out session, but take this as a dress rehearsal."

THE PUKE.

***EEEUUW.* TONGUE (HIS)** stimulates gag reflex **(YOURS).** Too much, too deep, too soon. Says, "Do you need me to hold your hair back?"

End of Date Bonus Round
THE GIRLFRIEND RECAP

As we've been alluding to all along, even the worst date is worth going on. **Why?** Because the worst dates make the best stories. They are the stuff legends are made of. In fact, you probably know about the hellish dates of friends of friends you've never met.

No matter what happened—whether it was all fine wine and caviar or Wiffle ball and flat tires—you must immediately log in with the ladies. How can you not do your duty and contribute to the great female storytelling tradition? And of course, you need your friends' feedback. The less well you know a guy, the more detail you need to convey to your panel of experts. Date someone for months, and all you need to report to your posse is, "We went to the movies." But when you hardly know Mr. New, everything he does—from the popcorn he orders without butter (repressed?) to whether he stays for the credits (stays awake after sex?)—is ripe for the hopper. You need your amigas to sift through the haze and define the meaning of your date's most-minute actions, like so:

YOU: "Well, the thing is, he buttered his first slice of bread, but not his second."

FRIEND: "Easy. He just broke up with someone. He's still fond of her, but he's ready to move on. Okay—did he have regular or decaf?"

After you run your date data through the friend-o-matic, you'll have a better sense of how to proceed. Their expert analysis will help you make your next critical decision: Do you cash in your chips, or do you play this puppy for another round? **Read on.**

GOING FOR SECONDS?

Your first date is over —
and it looks like he
made it through
the preliminary
audition.  When you first saw him, you
knew that he at least had "the look."
Then there was the first date:
The screen test. He came across as
somewhat convincing —and
not too loud. So far, so good,
but all this doesn't necessarily
mean he wins the part
of boyfriend in the feel-
good romantic comedy that is your life.

The second impression is **what will make or break him.** Maybe you were blinded by his pearly whites and baby blues the first time around. Now you get a chance to dig deeper. How long can he suppress his innate guyness and pretend to be a considerate, caring, thoughtful, and sensitive schmo—and how long do you want him to? When he lets his guard down, you'll get the real picture.

Ideally, of course, you'd have this himbo wrapped around one of your dainty fingers and would be free to lounge about on an inflatable recliner in your pool, daiquiri in one hand, phone in the other. Maybe you'd take one of the desperate phone calls of the poor lovesick chappy you had just seduced with your heady mix of beauty, brains, and sex appeal. Maybe you'd finish reading *Cosmo*, soaking up ultraviolets instead. **You call the shots, princess.**

Or maybe not.

Maybe that's a daydream you're having as you tote the portable phone with you into the shower so you're sure not to miss his call.
Get a grip, girl. Men humiliate us enough without our having to do it ourselves. If you like the greaseball, call him. No matter *who* started it. What are you worried about? That you are going to "scare" him? Well, sure, you might…if you call him up and tell him you'd like to wear his skin as a housecoat. But stick to the basics and you'll be fine. Even if he's not interested, he'll be flattered. Unless he's a complete troglodyte. And in that case, who needs him?

In any case, the worst thing that can happen is that you'll get dissed.

THE BIG DIS

Hold the phone. What do you mean, *dissed*? You're a girl, he's a guy... what the hell's the problem?

If anyone's doing any dissing here, it darn well better be *you*. No matter what. But a couple of dismal scenarios are possible here. The first is, you ask him out and he dings you. The other totally hideous, atrocious, unthinkable turn of events is that you, totally uninterested, don't call . . . and the vermin **has the *cojones* to actually call *you* and say that *he* doesn't think you should see each other anymore.**

Oh . . . my . . . Godfrey! Quick — reach for your . . .

EMERGENCY PRIDE SAVER

HERE'S WHAT YOU DO UPON HEARING THE FATEFUL WORDS:

1. IMMEDIATELY PLACE RECEIVER NEXT TO RUNNING HAIR DRYER.

2. YELL, "I CAN'T HEAR YOU. HANG ON — THIS CONNECTION SUCKS. GOTTA CHANGE CHANNELS. . . ."

3. TURN OFF HAIR DRYER.

4. SAY, "MUCH BETTER. ANYWAY, I'M GLAD YOU CALLED. I JUST WANTED TO TELL YOU, I THINK YOU ARE A REALLY NICE GUY AND ALL, BUT I'M REALLY NOT INTERESTED IN GOING OUT WITH YOU AGAIN. OH — THERE'S MY OTHER LINE!"

5. HANG UP.

Save! You've turned a potentially humiliating exchange into a triumph of the human spirit. You go, girl!

Luckily, you'll have to use this technique about as often as you'll have to use a butter churn. In most cases, you'll be **X'ondra, Demon Queen of Rejection, Fire-Belching Devourer of Puny Male Hearts.** Sometimes, though, the **great and powerful X'ondra shows mercy** and kills with kindness. Here are some of her techniques:

TYPE OF KISS-OFF	INTENTION
REVERSE PSYCHOLOGY	To actively scare him off with second date invitation.
ELABORATE SITCOM LIE	To cushion the blow by concocting a humongous fib that you and your friends have to go to madcap lengths to substantiate for the next three years.
NO-QUESTIONS-ASKED LIE	To cushion the blow by concocting a simple fib that hints at a gigantic problem.
THE INSANITY DEFENSE	Self-explanatory.
THE VANILLA ICE	To dump him in such a wishy-washy way that your spinelessness repulses him. He'll be off your case.
KID GLOVES	To cushion the blow because he's basically a nice guy.

EXAMPLE

"Y'know, instead of going to the movies, I think it would be more meaningful if you came over and acted out a dramatization of *The Bridges of Madison County* I've written. I've got your highlighted script all ready for you. How's sevenish sound?"

"Oh, you didn't go out with me. You went with my evil twin cousin, Pepper. I just hate it when she impersonates me. You can tell the difference between us because I always wear glasses and keep my hair in a bun. Plus her parents are much more lenient—mine don't let me date."

"Sorry, but I'm not allowed to date outside the Witness Protection Program."

"Sorry, I can't hear you very well on this phone—I'm getting a lot of interference. My fillings keep picking up these signals from Trondar 17. It's a Class D planet in the Hydroxian System—so I'm surprised it's coming in so clearly . . . Look, how 'bout I call you back?"

"You're a terrific guy. I think of you like a brother. But I'm not in a very 'relationship' place right now. I've named the problem; now I have to own it . . . on my own. It's meant a lot for me to share. Thanks a lot."

"Yeah, maybe a bunch of us can all hang out together sometime."

GAMES PEOPLE PLAY

Here's the way it should work:

DATE NO. 1 ▶ **PHONE CALL** ▶ **DATE NO. 2**

Unfortunately, it's not always that clean. Things get messy after your first trip to Six Flags over Walla Walla, because, after all, we have our pride. Neither one of you wants to look too eager, so consider the following

---

1. LET YOUR ROOMMATE ANSWER ALL PHONE CALLS.

This serves two purposes:
A) Allows for roommate input on his telephone manner and the timbre of his voice, and
B) Lets him know that you're not exactly waiting by the phone!

---

2. WARMLY DECLINE HIS FIRST INVITATION DUE TO FICTIONAL— AND ALLURING—SCHEDULING CONFLICT.

EXAMPLE: "Ooh, no can do. Saturday's totally booked. In the morning I have this audition to be Heather Locklear's body double, and then later I've got this stunt-pilot lesson."

---

3. LET HIM THINK HE HAS A LITTLE COMPETITION.

Drop in a reference to any other male in your life without identifying him as your father, brother, dog, etc.

EXAMPLE: "Yeah, the weather is great! Rex and I were just jogging in the park."

D DAY	FAT CHANCE	2ND CHANCE ✓

Thankfully, a few guys do deserve a second going-over. Even goddesses need to be entertained once in a while, and sometimes a Saturday night with the gals eating Fig Newtons and watching a very special *Blossom* rerun just won't do it for you. Who knows, maybe the man who took you to see the all-orca *Nutcracker* at Sea World is — dare we say it — potential boyfriend material. Maybe not.

Maybe he's just a lot of fun to hang around with.

In either case, no worries. A second date doesn't mean you are officially going steady or anything. It's a golden opportunity to see if he is going to relax his best-behavior standards a bit and slip up (now that he's a little more relaxed, if he calls you **"My Queen"** or **"Mommy,"** performs the theme from *The A-Team* for you in belches, or shows up for a beach trip in lime-green spandex shorts, you are out of there). Wherever you go for your second date, pay careful attention to his various character flaws.

Afterward, discuss them in detail with your friends, and after weighing his pluses and minuses, take the time to give yourself this little quiz:

WORTHINESS QUIZ

1. HE REMINDS ME OF:

A) myself

B) my father

C) my hamster

2. SOME OF THE THINGS WE HAVE IN COMMON ARE:

A) a childlike curiosity about the world around us, a zest for life, and a wicked sense of humor

B) shyness and a fear of having our hearts broken

C) warm blood and the ability to see colors

3. I CAN REALLY SEE US HAVING:

A) a picnic under the stars

B) a passionate argument about politics

C) a price on our heads

4. WHEN I AM WITH HIM I FEEL LIKE:

A) a princess

B) a little kid

C) a hostage

5. HE'S DIFFERENT FROM ALL THE OTHER GUYS BECAUSE:

A) he's not afraid to own up to his feelings

B) he's a one-woman man

C) he runs his own militia

6. I LIKE IT WHEN HE:

A) calls just to say hi

B) calls

C) falls for my roommate's lies about where I am

7. HE MAKES ME WANT TO:

A) sing

B) shout

C) move

8. HE'S IMPORTANT TO ME BECAUSE:

A) I've never met anyone like him

B) he provides an opportunity to see if I'm ready to date again

C) I need a ride

If you answered *C* to more than three of the above questions, you need to adjust your bikini, scramble up that high dive, and jump back into the dating pool. No more mercy dates: "Nice" girls finish with losers, you know. On the other hand, if this guy has passed this quiz with flying colors—or even if he slipped in under the wire—he might just deserve one more audience with Her Most Excellency the High Priestess of Hotitude.

5

"SO, UM, WHAT'S OUR DEAL?"

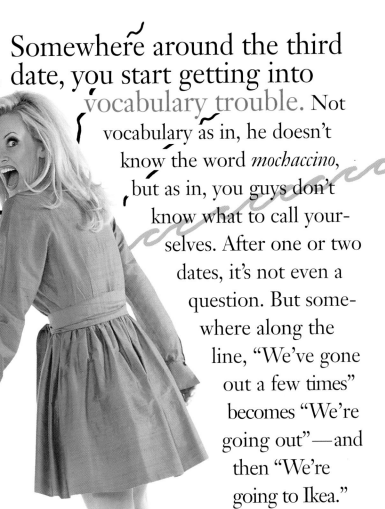

Somewhere around the third date, you start getting into vocabulary trouble. Not vocabulary as in, he doesn't know the word *mochaccino*, but as in, you guys don't know what to call yourselves. After one or two dates, it's not even a question. But somewhere along the line, "We've gone out a few times" becomes "We're going out"—and then "We're going to Ikea."

But when?

Things would be so easy if you were, say, Marcia Brady. She always knew exactly where she stood with Doug Simpson, Harvey Klinger, Desi Arnaz, Jr., and the gang. It was always either/or.

Either they went on **"a date"** *or* they were **"going steady."** Marcia would be quite sure if she was "going steady," because that would happen only if a boy said, "Marcia, would you like to go steady?" and she said **yes.**

If only. Problem is, not only are all these terms really fuzzy to begin with, but men and women don't always interpret them the same way.

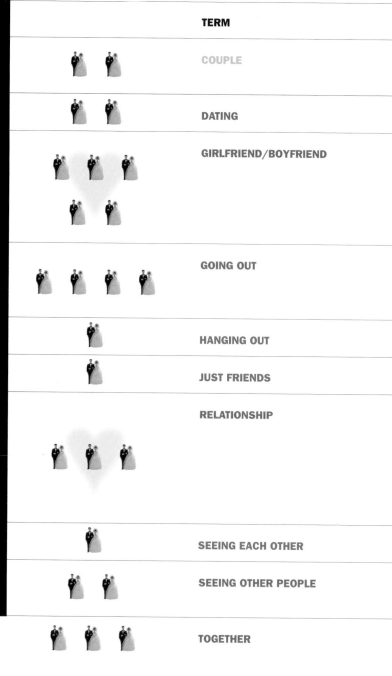

	TERM
	COUPLE
	DATING
	GIRLFRIEND/BOYFRIEND
	GOING OUT
	HANGING OUT
	JUST FRIENDS
	RELATIONSHIP
	SEEING EACH OTHER
	SEEING OTHER PEOPLE
	TOGETHER

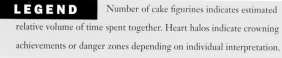

LEGEND Number of cake figurines indicates estimated relative volume of time spent together. Heart halos indicate crowning achievements or danger zones depending on individual interpretation.

What we have provided here is *the* authoritative dictionary of all of this dating language. Use it to decide which term best suits your changing situation.

DEFINITION

What you are as far as the general public is concerned if you appear together in broad daylight after sleeping together.

Going on dates, but allowed to see other people (see below).

Can be used only after at least five dates, if you have gone somewhere together for a weekend, or when a third party asks you the nature of your relationship. At that point you may say either, "Okay, I guess we are *girlfriend/boyfriend*" or, "We are just friends."

What you say when you have gone out more than three times but have not had the opportunity/courage to employ the term *girlfriend/boyfriend*.

Sleeping together.

See "Hanging Out."

The word he hates. Tell him to chill. It's not as a serious as he thinks. It is a catchall term covering everything from nightly candlelit dinners to the odd game of foosball. For example, "We play tennis once a month and hook up every once in a while—that's our *relationship*." Serious only when preceded by "in a" as in, "We've been in a *relationship* for ten years."

See "Hanging Out."

Either just starting to date, or no longer a couple. You are allowed to go on dates, but he is not.

A relationship that consists of making public appearances as a couple, as in, "You can't dance with Tony. He and Lola are *together*." Does not, however, indicate permanence. Lola and Rico could be together at another party the same week. Also not the same as "getting together," which refers to all initial erotic contact—as in "I met her at the Copa, and we ended up *getting together*." Getting together can lead to a *relationship*, or nothing at all.

Building a Love Shack

When you fall into a succession of one-night stands with the same person, all of a sudden they aren't one-night stands anymore. The way you know if you've graduated from "scamming" to "shacking" is that *shacking* means that you are no longer slipping into his apartment under cover of darkness and slinking out in the wee hours of the morning.

That means you are seeing his apartment during the day, which in turn means that you are going to have to deal with its interior, and its inhabitants, *with the lights on.*

Talk about a rude awakening: One morning, well after sunup, you'll open your eyes to **Martha Stewart's vision of hell.** You'll inhale a potpourri of stale Domino's and tube socks; you'll appreciate for the first time the craftsmanship of the room's centerpiece: a pyramid constructed entirely of beer cans.

Of course, there are some men who do stock their bathrooms with actual toilet paper rather than take-out napkins. But they, unfortunately, are in the minority. If you are ducking into his hut on a regular basis, come prepared with supplies: contact lens solution, soap, a clean cup, and maybe your own fork.

And don't forget your toothbrush. Any cad who offers you a **"girl" toothbrush** as part of his hospitality program is not so much considerate as grody. His last guest could have been Halitosa Jones, for goodness' sake.

But deep down, that guy means well. And that's kind of cute. You'd rather hang with someone a little clueless than someone whose bed has hospital corners, who follows you around with a dustpan, or who adjusts the positions of his knickknacks after you breathe on them (actually, you shouldn't trust a guy who has knickknacks in the first place). And besides, not every girl is Nancy Neatness to begin with — why, you might feel right at home among his woolly dust mammoths. Anyway, consult this chart to see how much you can put up with from the guy who puts you up:

HOME SWEET HOME	HOUSE OF HORRORS
He rents steamy foreign films for you.	He has a giant Foreigner poster.
He serves you his famous fettucine.	He serves you Spaghetti-O's over the sink.
He still sleeps with his Blanky.	He still wets his Blanky.
His room is filled with plants...	...that grew in his sink.
He puts his dirty clothes in the hamper...	...and selects his outfit from it the next day.
He invites you to bond with his roommates over an evening of parlor games.	The main event is Strip Pictionary.
He takes good care of his pet...	...silverfish.

Hanging with His Friends:
THREE THINGS YOU NEED TO KNOW

LESSON NO. 1: YOU DON'T HAVE TO BE "A GUY."

Guys like girls, remember? No need to go into scratch-and-sniff mode to get in with the crowd. Yes, they'll like you if you understand the nuances of championship BMX racing, but they'll like you just as much—if not better—if you allow them to explain it to you.

LESSON NO. 2: THEY DON'T KNOW THAT MUCH ABOUT YOU.

Your friends know everything about him: briefs vs. boxers; his favorite song; what his sister does for a living. His friends know nothing. They're not bad people, and it's not that they don't care, but the fact is that they simply lack the brain lobe that retains biographical information about their friends' dates. He could have said, "Now, behave, you guys, I'm bringing home this really cool girl, Sniffany, heiress to the Kleenex fortune," and by the time you get there, they'll be like, "So, what do you do?"

LESSON NO. 3: THEY'RE EASY TO PLEASE.

Just be yourself. No need to win them over by becoming Den Mother. Swooping in with Pine-Sol, covering their furniture with plastic, and leaving perfumed pink Post-its thanking them for their hospitality may not have the desired effect. In fact, they may mutiny and inform your new squeeze: "Either the Wilma goes, or we do."

Once you two kids have been going out for a while, you may face **another big test** in your **quest** for **love's Holy Grail.** Spending a weekend away together will try your **fortitude, patience,** and **compatibility** like nothing you have faced so far.

A vacation can be a pretty heavy trip for a new couple. Here's where you find out who really folds the map in this relationship. If you make it back from your romantic getaway without having to get away from each other, you're in good shape.

The secret to a bicker-free vacation is all in knowing what to expect. To smooth out your ride, consult this guide to the highways, byways, and guy-ways that you'll face along the way to Playa de Pressure. And if your trip looks anything like the one below, congratulations. You're normal.

STOP NO. 1

TRAVEL TOWN

You hit this store like Hurricane Hilda, scooping up guidebooks, maps, bug spray, granola bars, fruit roll-ups, diet soda, and handy-wipes while he's home packing. Oh, wait. He's not. He'll just toss a dirty T-shirt and a Gameboy into his knapsack on his way out the door.

STOP NO. 2

THE OPEN ROAD

Here's where the heat under your collars hits the highway. His driving sucks, but you can't say anything "critical." He refuses to consult a map, look at road signs, or stop for anything but an engine fire. You argue, then ride along in chilly silence.

STOP NO. 3

CUTE BED 'N' BREAKFAST (YOUR IDEA)

Creaky bed.

STOP NO. 4

MORNING WARNING

He wants to sleep in until three ("It's a vacation!"), and you want to make the first tour of the Fortress of Solitude ("It's historic!"). You spit insults at each other while waiting for your complimentary huevos rancheros.

STOP NO. 5

CRAZY EDUARDO'S SOUVENIR SHACK

Truce. You allow him to purchase the *grande* size Dallas Cowboys Superbowl XXX commemorative piñata. *If* he will wait for you to write and mail thirty postcards.

STOP NO. 6

HOME AGAIN, HOME AGAIN

So, was your long weekend nice — or just plain *long*? If the very sight of him makes you want to hightail it to the safety of your hacienda, your passport to Loveland may soon expire. But if, after being trapped together for a whole weekend, you still want to hang, you may have hit the frequent-flier-mile jackpot on Trans Atlantic Boyfriend. That certainly bodes well.

Meeting His Family
THE MOTHERS OF ALL BOYFRIENDS

He wets his pants at the very thought of shooting the breeze with your folks (or does he? See "Coping with Her Clan," page 77 ♂). You, on the other hand, are **dying of curiosity about his family.** It's all a part of your fact-finding process, regardless of what you want out of the relationship. Inquiring minds want to know what his **baby pictures** look like.

When you do get the chance to celebrate the **Fourth of July** over at his family manse, your main objective is to **observe his mother.** Pay no attention to the man behind the barbeque. The father is irrelevant to your investigation. Nice guy maybe, but a total nonstarter when it comes to deciphering your companion's character. How your man relates to his mommy gives a sense of how you can expect him to treat you over the next few weeks and months.

How Does He Treat His Mom
THE SON SCREEN

HE LIKES HER

GOOD GUY. This is a guy who never forgets her birthday or anniversary. Not a bad sign.

MAMA'S BOY. Uh-oh. This is a guy who never forgets his mother's shopping list. Um, boundaries?

HE DOESN'T LIKE HER

OPPOSITES ATTRACT. He'll look to you for everything she isn't. If she's Mrs. Cleaver, he'll hope you're Mrs. Bundy. Or vice versa.

WOMAN-HATER.
CAUTION. He thinks all women are Mrs. Bundy.

Holiday In Hell

Presents: We want them, we like them, and we're great at giving them. Usually. The only time we get tripped up is when a relationship is in its tender infancy. If you met him two weeks ago, and it's suddenly Valentine's Day, his birthday, or National Muffler Day, you're in a tough spot. It may be too soon for boxes and bows, but you can't not get him anything — that would be setting a bad example.

So, what do you do? You have to make some token acknowledgment of his special day. Something simple and sweet. No pressure on you or him. You know, a little homemade card, peanut butter cookies, a hand-chiseled ice sculpture of a 1965 Mustang with a brand new muffler. Use this nifty personal shopping tool to decide whether he'll react to your gesture with "Oh, you shouldn't have . . . " or "Uh, you *shouldn't* have. . . . "

CUTE	SCARY
Buy him a bunny.	Cook it.
Bake him cookies.	Lace them with Love Potion No. 9.
Make him a card.	Make your own paper.
Buy him a book.	Write him a book.
Call him on his birthday.	Call his mother on his birthday.
Send him flowers.	Send him a stripper.
Send him an e-mail.	Send him a she-male.
Buy him a CD.	Buy him a CD-ROM.
Clean up his kitchen.	Knock out a wall.
Buy him a single chocolate kiss.	Jump out of a chocolate cake.

Congratulations. You've swum through some of the choppiest waters in the dating pool; weathering a fashion crisis, unlocking the secrets of strange male rituals, risking rejection, and enduring plagues of dweebs. But guess what–just because you've mastered the finer points of flirting and the dynamics of dissing doesn't mean you get to haul yourself up on the medal podium just yet. Even when you've got a special someone on your car phone's speed dial, you still have plenty of stormy, cramp-inducing, dizzying seas to navigate. And just because you are cruising along with the same stud for more than two weekends in a row doesn't mean you have to wear a strand of his belly button hair in a locket around your neck.

THE END? Play it by ear. You can keep or dump him. If you keep him, best of luck. And if you dump him, see page one.

ING

By J.D. Heiman

Produced by
Melcher Media

Designed by
Alexander Isley Design

MTV Books/PocketBooks/Melcher Media

Love stinks. Sometimes it sucks.

But you can't let that stop you. Despite all those misses, there are some real hits out there just waiting for you to step up with just the right look and just the right line at just the right time.

Not that your hormones would let you sit out the game, anyway. Hit any scam shack on a weekend night and you'll enter a mosh pit of lust-crazed desperadoes who, just like you, are all competing for the fiercest females in the joint.

Of course, you surrender to that primal urge to find the perfect mate to invite back to your lair. What else can you do? Loaf around at home every Saturday night for private screening of *Beastmaster V: Love Slaves of the Amazon Army*?

Well, maybe every other Saturday.

Most of the time, though, you gotta be out there, **prowling for that special someone** to warm the furs.

But how should you choose the best of the bunch, chat her up with a little finesse, and show her you like her? Your path is filled with pitfalls: **Insecurity, Rejection, Fatal Attraction the 13th...** Plus, you've got to outmaneuver all the other dudes at the bar, club, party, Stop 'n' Shop—whatever—to get to the right babe first. And then how do you hit it off *with* her when everyone else is hitting *on* her?

You need to be the one who catches her eye—without blindsiding her.

This book will show you **the right way to pick and pursue the choicest chicas out there.** We're heading deep into the trenches of the war between the sexes to send back dispatches on where to look, what to wear, whom to ditch, why to arrive ten minutes late, and — God help you — how to dance.

We'll find out **whether we have anything in common with women at all,** except this burning yearning urge to play Naked Twister (and, okay, to have someone sweet to keep you cozy at night).

So pull on those trunks, buddy, check that drawstring, and hustle up to the high-dive. **It's time for you to cannonball into the dating pool.**

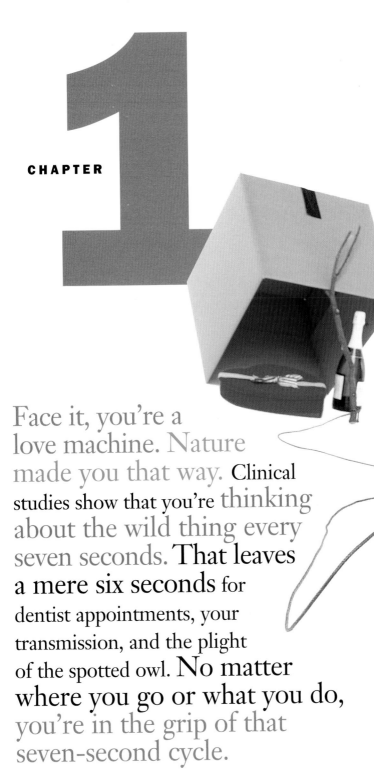

Face it, you're a
love machine. Nature
made you that way. Clinical
studies show that you're thinking
about the wild thing every
seven seconds. That leaves
a mere six seconds for
dentist appointments, your
transmission, and the plight
of the spotted owl. No matter
where you go or what you do,
you're in the grip of that
seven-second cycle.

BUILDING YOUR PERFECT FRANKENBABE

THE MEAT MARKET

Building Your Perfect Frankenbabe

AGE	*A)* The Olsen twins *B)* Alicia Silverstone *C)* Florence Henderson
BRAIN	*A)* Sydney from *Melrose Place* *B)* Tabitha Soren *C)* Daria from Beavis & Butt-head
SENSITIVITY	*A)* Courtney Thorne-Smith *B)* Courteney Cox *C)* Courtney Love
LOOKS	*A)* Tori Spelling *B)* Shannen Doherty *C)* Jennie Garth
BUTT	*A)* Kate Moss *B)* Suzanne "Butt Master" Somers *C)* Sally Struthers
HAIR	*A)* Jennifer Aniston *B)* Vanessa Williams *C)* Sinéad O'Connor
HUMOR	*A)* Ellen DeGeneres *B)* Ellen Cleghorne *C)* Eleanor Roosevelt
TEN YEAR PLAN	*A)* Master's Degree *B)* Mrs. Degree *C)* Mistress
CHEST	*A)* Sierra Nevadas *B)* Hollywood Hills *C)* Death Valley

But you can't let your demon hormones run your life. Give in to the dark side of desire and last night's Lamborghini may turn into this morning's lemon. You have to have standards — even ideals — when you're looking around.

Now, that doesn't mean you have to **take a vow of celibacy** until you meet Miss Perfect. It just means that when you think about **getting hot and heavy,** you need to *think about it,* or you risk being outwitted by some wily woman-thing. Set some standards, control those impulses, and plan ahead. Sure, your dream girl may not exist in this dimension, but this quiz will help kick your brain into the proper gear.

THERE'S ONLY ONE JENNY MCCARTHY

MAKING YOUR IDEAL REAL

"Find a friend first—most purely-physical relationships don't last. When all else fails, you'll still have a friend." —*James, 21*

Well done, Dr. Date. You've patched together the perfect Babenstein. But do you have what it takes to bring her to life? Some nights, you might actually catch a glimpse of that comely creature. Others, though, will be all-night creature features. Look, there's only **one set of Jenny McCarthy DNA,** and chances are, it's not looking for you.

Chat up a less-than-fetching individual when your hormones are slam-dancing in your pants, and you may be screening your phone calls for the next three weeks. **Here's the dilemma:** Your plumbing says, "Hook up ... with *anybody*," but your pride says, "Except her."

Smart scopers know how to spot the different kinds of female packaging. And in fact, women tend to make this easy for us. They seem to feel compelled to present themselves in handy prefab types.

So while you should definitely keep an open mind, you need to narrow your search. **Don't waste your time** prowling the wrong corner of passion's jungle. Use this handy girl-guide to weed your way through the prospects.

Handy Girl Guide

HIPPIE CHICK

UNIFORM: Stitched together with natural fibers from several developing countries.
SCENT: Patchouli and BO.
SHOES: Optional.
HOBBIES: Weaving, carob.
ROLE MODEL: Joni Mitchell.
Says things like, "I feel this powerful energy between us, so you can spend the night in my sleeping bag. But I want you to know that I'm not quite over Jerry." A real free spirit, but don't go through customs with her.

VAMPIRA

UNIFORM: Black lipstick, spiderweb tattoos on hands.
HOBBIES: Morrissey, death.
ROLE MODEL: Siouxsie Sioux.
Dresses like Dracula, but doesn't eat meat. Beach volleyball is not an option — prefers "role-playing games" to spectator sports and sunlight.

Says things like, "Saturday's out. I've been waiting since the solstice for Anne Rice's book signing and séance." Working knowledge of the occult freaks out your parents. Dump her and she's got a voodoo doll with your name on it.

RIOT GRRL
UNIFORM: Little vintage dress, steel-toed boots.
HAIR: Don't even think about touching it.
HOBBIES: Anarchist bowling league, blowing up the trucks that deliver the Swimsuit Issue to newsstands.
ROLE MODEL: The chick in Bikini Kill who beat up Courtney Love.
Says things like, "Hey, Dog Boy, wanna catch a Lunachicks concert? I'll let you ride shotgun." She's great, if you want to go out with a gal who's not afraid to engage in belching or Indian wrestling contests. Rest assured, this chick can back you up in a knife fight.

STRAWBERRY SHORTCAKE
UNIFORM: Think pink.
HOBBIES: Needlepoint, caring for the less fortunate, collecting stickers, making killer peach cobbler.
ROLE MODEL: Amy Grant.
Says things like, "This pin, shaped like the pot of gold at the end of the rainbow, represents a special pledge that I shall keep until marriage." Your mother loves her; hers wants her back by 9:30 P.M.

BIONIC WOMAN
UNIFORM: Ankle weights, Chapstick, Lycra, Tevas.
HAIR: Ponytail yanked through back of baseball cap.
HOBBIES: Ice climbing, whitewater rafting, sea kayaking, the Iditarod.
ROLE MODEL: Picabo Street.
Says things like, "Whoo-hoo! [pant, pant] That triathlon was suh-weet!" Sports goggle-tan year-round. A plaque hangs in her honor at Patagonia world headquarters. She's cute, but you have to go through basic training to keep up with her.

DITSY MITZI

UNIFORM: Tall hair, held in place by huge pink plastic object.

HOBBIES: Lip gloss, looking for her car keys, collecting different colored highlighters.

ROLE MODEL: "Um, you know, those girls that come out in the cute outfits at the basketball game—what are their names again?" Says things like, "Ha ha ha! [pause] Um, I don't get it!" May not actually be *that* dumb—poor soul confuses acting like an idiot with sexy flirting technique. Guaranteed to make you feel like a rocket scientist for a while, then annoy the hell out of you.

MOODY TRUDY

UNIFORM: Bathrobe, tissues, frozen yogurt.

HOBBIES: Nail-biting, snipping old boyfriends out of pictures. You only meet her when her friends drag her away from the VCR because she "needs to get out and meet new people."

ROLE MODEL: Cathy. Says things like, "Ha ha! [frowns] That's not funny." She's up, she's down, and you're all over the place. Get used to saying these magic words: "Why are you crying?"

GOLDEN GIRL

UNIFORM: Sweater with sparkly things on it, monogrammed eyewear.

HAIR: Stiff, brass-colored.

ROLE MODEL: Joan Rivers. Bitter chicken hawk swooping back into dating scene after messy divorce. Says things like, "You got nice, tight buns, Junior. Just like my second husband—the bastard," in raspy voice indicating two-decade Virginia Slims habit. Has a Jacuzzi, but you'll have to put up with the Chippendales posters.

MADAME CURIE

UNIFORM: Triple-strapper—always keeps backpack securely fastened on both shoulders and around waist.

SHOES: "Sensible."

HOBBIES: Archery, madrigals, moderating "alt.fan.geometry" newsgroup on Internet.

ROLE MODEL: Copernicus.

Says things like, "No, no, no! Chekov was the navigator. *Sulu* was the helmsman." Doesn't get out much, but if you take the time to get to know her, you may ignite a Bunsen burner of repressed passion.

MADAM PRESIDENT

UNIFORM: Electronic organizer, shoulder pads.

HOBBIES: Community action, internships, seminars, workshops, rewriting résumé.

ROLE MODEL: Bill Gates.

Says things like, "I can fit you in for a breakfast meeting the last Thursday of next month, from 7:30 to 8:00 A.M. We can talk then about what you'd bring to any future association with me." You fear her.

TRENDY WENDY

UNIFORM: Whatever Daisy Fuentes is wearing.

HOBBIES: Weird shoes, obscure bands, changing her hair.

ROLE MODEL: The supermodels.

Says things like, "I was so disappointed in Christy Turlington's outfit—those espadrilles are, like, so five minutes ago." High maintenance/low tolerance honey demands cutting-edge dude to escort her to series of after-hours clubs where she can analyze celebrity skirt lengths and lapel widths. You usually have to drive—her Jetta is crammed with designer shopping bags.

TRUST FUND TRIXIE

UNIFORM: Pearls, headband, horse.

HOBBIES: Fox hunting, collecting interest.

ROLE MODEL: The Daughters of the American Revolution.

Says things like, "Bunky, Bitsy, Bunny, Bootsie, Twinkie, and I are planning a charity croquet cotillion at the club. Would you care to be my escort? Of course, it's black-tie. Daddy will send a car." This blue-blooded babe sometimes strays from the social register set. If you are up to being her downtown boy, she may take you to grandpapa's plantation on St. Bart's.

SUITING UP
FOR BATTLE

> "I went on my *Singled Out* date with two outfits in a garment bag, including my beige Armani two-piece. It always pays to be prepared." — *Ronald*, 24

> "Wear a denim shirt with khakis — that's sort of a mid-casual feel. If you need to spruce it up, add a tie. That way you've got a higher form of dressy, but still casual." — *James*, 21

> "There's a guy at this club who wears a vinyl vest with no shirt. I'm like, did you forget something?" — *Leah*, 18

> "One thing I'll never understand is that vest-with-no-shirt look." — *Abby*, 21

Women don't judge you by your labels, but they do judge you by your look. While clothes don't necessarily make the man, they do make or break the first impression. Show up looking like an unmade bed and you may not see someone else's for a long time.

(And to you skivey dirtbags out there — you know who you are — take a shower. A fresh coat of deodorant doesn't count.)

Here's the catch. While you do have to pay attention to your looks, you don't want it to look like you pay so much attention that girls will think you have no attention left for, say, a girlfriend. Dressing "sexy" on purpose is a mistake. Show up in something straight out of Siegfried and Roy's walk-in closet and you'll be slurping piña coladas all by your gelled-up lonesome. You have to find that critical middle ground between **pig boy and** peacock.

Think of yourself as a walking version of your apartment. A Spaghetti-O-splattered Rush shirt says, **"I have a Spaghetti-O-splattered apartment with a Rush bedspread."** And **nothing says** **"mirrors on the ceiling, leopard-skin wallpaper, and Barry White on the hi-fi"** like the ol' double-breasted shiny suit with a mother lode of ore around your neck. Get the picture? She'll never come home with you if one glance tells you're squatting in Satan's duplex.

(From this standpoint, the only risk of looking clean, coordinated, and tucked-in is that your outfit might say, "I live with my mom.")

You know better than to **wear anything visibly dirty** (or at least now you do). Besides, you may already have a going-out uniform. Yep, a Get-Lucky Shirt. Sure you do. It's probably a denim button-down or a plaid flannel. You know the one . . . and so does she. It's the nice big cuddly shirt that **she pictures herself wearing in the morning, sleeves rolled up and with nothing underneath,** while she scrambles eggs for two. Don't have one? Get one.

Unfortunately, not every guy knows how smart it is to keep things so simple. When you get out there, it may look as if your plain blue oxford has some flashier competition. But does it? Here's the run-down on those goobers and what their clothes say to womankind.

PAPER DOLL WARDROBE

PAPER DOLL 1: CATALOG BOY
ROLE MODEL: Calvin Klein.
Never shops in stores, but checks out his reflection in the windows when he walks by.
SAYS: "This shirt isn't blue, it's Aegean Dusk."

PAPER DOLL 2: RAVE BOY
ROLE MODEL: The guy from Radiohead.
The swirly strobe lights are on, but nobody's home. When "the scene" vanishes, so will he.
SAYS: "Oooh, look at the pretty colors. . . ."

PAPER DOLL 3: CLAM-DIGGER BOY
ROLE MODEL: The residents of Animal House.
Women worry that he'll spill his dip cup on their front seat.
SAYS: "Can't go with pants, can't go with shorts. Afraid of commitment. Hey, I think I'll wear these clam-diggers."

PAPER DOLL 4: ROCKER BOY
ROLE MODEL: Tommy Lee.
His hair makes or breaks him: Women will put up with his tight gray jeans if he's got a big, thick mane. No stringiness will be tolerated.
SAYS: (upon seeing Tarty Party Girl (see page 18 ♀): "Schwing!"

PAPER DOLL 5: CAPITALIST-TOOL BOY
ROLE MODEL: G. Gordon Liddy.
She worries that even if she gets him down to his tighty whities, he'll insist on leaving his black socks on.
SAYS: "Your eyes go with my power tie. May I buy you a Scotch? Thank you for your consideration."

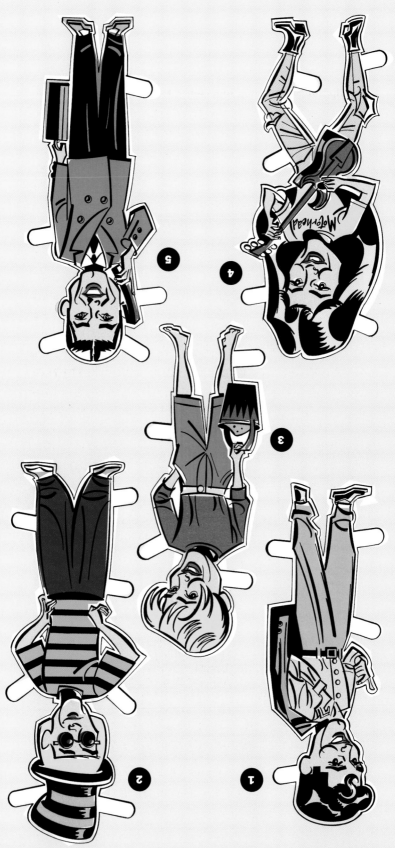

FINDING YOUR PREY
IN ITS NATURAL HABITAT

"Stay away from club girls." —*David, 24*

"People don't go to clubs to start rela-tionships. They go to clubs to start one-night stands." —*Chris, 18*

"I usually meet girls in clubs." —*Mark, 21*

Sure, you could **take the easy way out and hit the clubs. At Scam-o-Rama** the pickins are never slim, and some of the ice is already broken. Everyone there knows exactly why everyone else is there. You don't have to pretend that you're actually interested in how she keeps busy; you both know that all that small talk is just filler before you *get* busy.

But that scene, boy-o, is strictly amateur. Way too easy. **Clubs are for cubs.** The king of the jungle prowls elsewhere — and everywhere. His senses, much more finely tuned, are able to sniff out the finest impala. Not when they're all herded into one room and on their guard, but when they're in their most natural—and most unsuspecting—state.

Point is, you need to get a little more creative. Go to the places she goes, where she does the things she does—her natural habitat. When you meet a girl in natural light, you'll get a better sense of who she is, minus the spackle she coats herself in before heading out to Singles Space. And if you play your cards right, she won't think of you as the drooling hyena you are at heart. Here's how to pick up her trail.

LEGEND

THE KINGDOM OF SCAM-A-LOT. More girls than you can shake your little black book at.

THE REPUBLIC OF CHICK-O-SLOVAKIA. Mixed bag of Bettys here. Try your luck.

THE SKANK-A-MONICA PIER. Your last resort. You never know, but you'll probably end up taking a long walk off this short dating dock.

THE MALL

The mall is Girl Central, but whom you meet there depends on where you look. Skip the PSAT set in the food court drooling over their new Jamie Walters CDs and dodge the *Matlock* set power-walking the perimeter for their daily constitutional. Instead, head for where the hottest tamales hang: Garter Belts 'R' Us, Bikini Hut, and Organica Natural Dolphin-Safe/Not-Tested-on-Animals Bath and Beauty Boutique.

DON'T FORGET: A surefire flirting technique is to head for a clothing store and act clueless. Helpful and fetching retail bunnies will descend upon you offering their expert knowledge of clothing cuts and colors other than blue. Even if you don't get a date, they'll boost your ego in order to boost their commissions.

COMPARISON SHOPPING:

THREE GROCERY STORES, THREE TYPES OF GIRL.

SAFE-MART

Get your frosted minibutt out of the cereal aisle and over to **fresh produce, whole grains, and free-range fauna.** Forget your true foraging habits—that's where she'll be scoping for you (see "Groceryland," 21 ♀). If you need to look like you fit in, simply pick up two packages and appear to compare them. Maybe she'll lend a hand . . . ?

SNOBUCCI'S GOURMET GROCERY

PROPS: One baguette (french bread), one bottle olive oil (extra-virgin). Carry these under your arm and you'll look like you know what you're doing. Good place to run into **Trust Fund Trixie** or **Trendy Wendy.**

STOP, GUZZLE 'N' GO

If you're willing to keep pulling off the interstate in search of **a girl who knows her way under a car hood,** more power to ya. But you'll probably wind up nursing a Blizzard solo.

TONE 'N' TAN SPORTS & FITNESS CENTER

YOUR MISSION, SHOULD YOU CHOOSE TO ACCEPT IT: Take aerobics. We are not kidding. This will distinguish you from the throngs of thong-gazers steaming up the observation windows. If you **take up position at the rear of the room, they can't analyze your form—but you can analyze theirs.**

HARDBODY BEACH
As far as quality control goes, **basically an outdoor bar.** After all, it's a public place. Unless you've got a pass to David Hasselhoff's private cove, you'll be sharing the sand with—well, everybody. No challenge at all. But if you do go, **you may want to stop off at Clean 'n' Jerks Gym before you bare your chest.**

SORORITY ROW AT STATE U.
Hordes of unattached Greek goddesses whiling away long lonely hours baking fudge brownies and organizing visits to nursing homes while house matron Mrs. Garrett guards the door. A total girl grab-bag—make it a quality venture simply by learning the difference between Sigma Babe and Kappa Dogma.

THE COLLEGE OF OUR LADY OF PERPETUAL FRUSTRATION
There are at least two kinds of gals up at Perpetual: Those who **follow the ways of the Madonna** and those who **follow the ways of Madonna.** It just might be worth crashing their spring break tea dance.

MICHAEL BOLTON CONCERT AT THE COLISEUM
Keep your eyes peeled for the source of the **flying undies** (Golden Girl, that is).

BOOK NOOK
PROP: Book, glasses if possible. A book in your hand—unless it's *The World's Funniest Sports Bloopers Pop-up*—**makes you instantly sensitive, safe, and smart.** More so than a football, anyway. You can feel comfortable approaching any browsing Bitsy and saying, "So, what books are on your nightstand?"

TCB (TONS OF CHICKS BUYING) YOGURT
An eternal smorgasbord: Triple-swirl-lickin', sprinkle-snarfin', **fat-free spandex-clad sweeties.** Plant yourself by the spoons and wait.

STOCKHOLM INTERNATIONAL MASSAGE THERAPY INSTITUTE
Meet the **woman of your muscles' dreams here.** But hey there, son, make sure it's accredited and that the word *parlor* doesn't appear in the name.

Babies and Puppies

Borrow someone else's moppet or mongrel for the day and suddenly you are Velcro for girl-lint. Women think you are promising man-material if you appear able to look after some creature other than yourself. So head for the Piggly Wiggly or the park, slyly let the kid or dog off the leash, and let him wander in the direction of an unsuspecting female. Sit back and watch her come to you.

EXCEPTIONS: If you are the father of the child, or if the dog is a killer pit bull, forget about it. And walking your pet gecko may draw the wrong kind of attention.

> "A good place to meet someone real is a place that is part of everyday life, like a grocery store. There, nobody is putting on an act. But first lines are pretty limited: 'So, grocery shopping, are ya?'" — *David, 24*

PSYCHING YOURSELF UP

After you've **run through our dating gauntlet,** you're ready to get out there and find the smooching **partner of your wildest dreams.** Nobody runs into Elle Macpherson while sitting on the recliner collecting belly button lint. Actually, there's no guarantee you'll run into Elle Macpherson at all, but that's not the point. Would you rather throw back microwaved chicken pot pies and drool over *Charlie's Angels* reruns all night or find a carbon-based angel of your very own? True, when you shove your face into a complete stranger's personal space, there's no telling if it's going to wind up decorated with beer foam, lipstick, or a hand print.

But you can't score from the sidelines, bub. Sure, it takes guts, but you gotta get out there. If you don't get off your butt, you'll never get a piece of anyone else's. And the more practiced you become at the love game, the more play you'll get.

Need we say more? Now hit the showers!

CHAPTER 2

It's one thing to locate her natural habitat. It's another thing entirely to act natural yourself when you're there. You can fake your knowledge of literature or latte for only so long.

So if you're not up to doing that much homework, you might consider the standard safety zone: The party. For most people, it's actually an unnatural habitat—too many humans in a hot room with plastic cups in their hands—but that's also why it's so easy, at least at the beginning. Everyone at a party is fair game (unless she's slow-dancing with Bruno to "Freebird"). But once you spy your little spinderella, things do get a little more complicated. Is she available? Is she interested? Is she interesting?

Is that toss of the head a
sexy come-on or
a cry for help
to her friends?
There's only one
way to find out.

NO

PUTTING THE MOVES

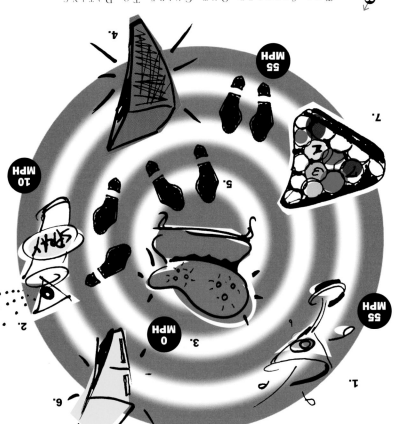

Walking into a party can be like para- chuting behind enemy lines.

WORKING THE ROOM

When you enter a room full of strangers, there's no telling precisely where under the dance floor the land mines are buried. You have no idea if that cutie by the guacamole is friend or foe. Don't be one of those lost boys wandering around the room wondering, **Where the hell are my friends?** or, **Is my fly unzipped?** The more you hem and haw with your hands jammed in your pocket, checking out the host's CD collection, **the more you morph into Dorkman.** And besides, you are a sitting duck for any desperate character looking to corner someone for an all-night lecture on his complete *Return of the Jedi* action figure collection. If you looked lame before, you'll look way lamer with that Ewok glued to your side.

A firm plan of action will help you avoid that kind of ambush — and allow you to enter the kingdom of **Babe-a-Lonia.** Use this map to plot your successful campaign.

1. FOOD TABLES/BAR

Source of . . . dinner. Also refills. Food and drink may provide conversation starters. But for same reason, bad hiding place. In general, limit pit stops to five minutes or you'll get pegged as "Still Here, Huh?" man.

IMPORTANT NOTE: You are what you eat. So stick to safe snacks. If you aren't careful, you'll be working the room with a Tang mustache, South-of-the-Border Nachos Fiesta breath, and Cheetos fingertips. Use your tongue to dislodge an impacted Jujyfruit from between your molars, and whomever you're chatting up will think you're making some creepy proposition.

2. BATHROOM/LINE FOR BATHROOM

Plenty of women here . . . but they're moving targets. Also, steer clear of the door; it may disgorge up to six women at once.

3. COUCH/SEATING AREA

CON: Black hole for socially challenged.

PRO: Likely retreat for shy Icelandic exchange student.

4. STEREO/BAND

In the world of parties, this neutral zone is a Switzerland. This is a good place to chill while licking your wounds or planning your next move. While you're parked there, feign an educated interest in the sound check or in your host's Supertramp anthology.

5. DANCE FLOOR

Be afraid. Be very afraid. (See "Dancin' Fools" page 28 ♂).

6. KITCHEN

Dearth of girls (unflattering light).

7. POOL TABLE

Pool game = girl magnet.

When it comes to shaking a leg, gentlemen, let's face it: Most of us suck. Sure, for some hotshots it comes naturally. If you're one of those guys who can really shake your thang, well, you hit the jackpot in the gene lottery. Fortunately, many of the rest of us can be trained to be as inoffensive as possible out on the floor.

But no matter what your skill level, as far as meeting women goes, **dancing is often a necessary evil**— and it beats having to talk. (It's not that women are thrilled about dancing with you, either. Apparently, they prefer to form a **ritual bonding circle** around a pile of sacrificial purses and shoes.)

Now, you don't have to look like **someone out of _Saturday Night Fever_,** but you don't want to look like **something out of _Friday the 13th._** Here's what you do (and don't worry—we won't tell anybody). Borrow your little sister's Ace of Base, take your walkman and this book into the bathroom, shut the door and lock it. Now hit play and put on your boogie shoes. If your choreography appears to match that of any of the offenders below, consider attending your next party with your foot in a cast ("Oh, this? Navy Seal rescue"). **Otherwise, just keep shaking that booty and praying that the speakers blow.** Listen to the music and try to find that beat. Keep your elbows below your shoulders at all times.

And whatever you do, don't spin.

SAFETY TIP: If you hear the opening bars of any Madonna song, run for cover to avoid being trampled by the **inevitable chick stampede.**

" If a woman is dancing with her girls, she either has a man or doesn't want to be bothered." — *Seth, 24*

THE LEGION OF DANCING DOOM

Hey! Watch It!

SPASTIC MAN

Armed and dangerous. This chicken is only funky until someone loses an eye.

EIGHTIES MAN

No, he's not looking for his contact lens, he's *breakin'*.

JUNIOR HIGH MAN

FEET: Nearly imperceptible left-right shuffle.

ARMS: Air guitar serves as boner shield.

Ouch, That's My Hand!

GROOVY MAN

Creating his own world with swirly-twirly hand movements. Interpretive dance symbolizes endless cycle of birth, death, and renewal.

Look Out, Disco Duck!

HEADBANGER MAN

Brings lighter; ignites hair.

JITTERBUG MAN

Delusions of dancing grandeur. Exuberantly applies ballroom dancing techniques to contemporary music, often yanking victim's arms out of sockets.

HIP-HOP GO-AWAY MAN

Brian Austin Green alert! Yo, uncross those arms, young man, and put your cap on straight. Peace.

LEECH MAN

Shimmies up behind unsuspecting female dancers, often suctioning his chest to victim's back. **Girls hate this.**

> "Sometimes what we do at clubs is dance around a group of girls, and then start dancing with them." —*Mark, 21*

Drafting Your Pals

You could hurl yourself into the dating void solo, but we don't recommend it. Where would Starsky be without Hutch, Ren without Stimpy, Dr. Dre without Ed Lover? The message is: Don't go in without backup. Here's how to get play with a little help from your friends.

SACRIFICIAL LAMB

Here's the situation. You see the woman of your dreams grabbing a fruity cooler from the fridge. The only problem is, your play is being blocked by some Heinous Hannah in a muumuu and a neck brace. Someone has got to run interference or you are going to waste all your energy fending off the guard dog.

That's where your friend comes in. He can play a round of Dungeons & Dragons with the muumuu mama while you get to know Daisy Duke better. What a guy (but remember, you'll owe him).

THE BODYGUARD

You'll feel less nervous when you go in with reinforcements. At the very least, you'll have someone to complain to when you get dissed (who else is going to say those soothing words "Don't worry about it, man—she wasn't worth it anyway . . ."?). Friends are great for ego-boosting, and not bad as human shields, either. You never know when you may need another body to block a hurled projectile or two.

PEER OPPRESSOR

Pressure from your friends keeps you all out there in the ongoing contest of **hookup-manship. The only problem is,** the more friends you have along when you're trolling, the more pressure there is for you to catch something. **Every move you make is being watched and judged.**

Heck, you all might as well hold up scorecards. There's nothing worse than having the **nudge-nudge-wink-wink posse** snickering within earshot when you are trying to get to know someone. What's more, **these people never forget anything.** Not the million times you've been rejected cold, and certainly not the freak shows you've wound up with on occasion. **Also very important:** One look at a gang of more than five guys moving as a pack and a woman can think only one thing:

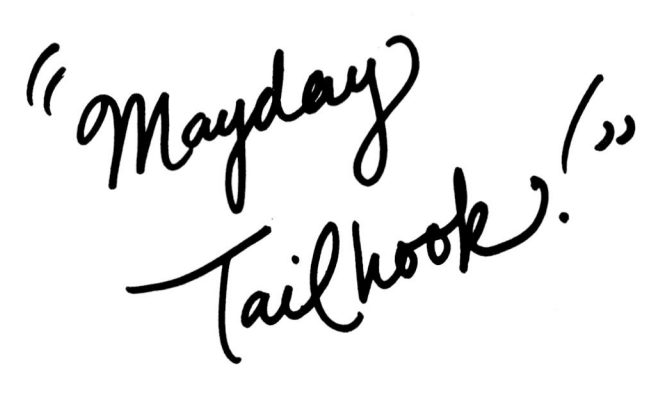

So the trick is, bring the squadron along for that much-needed moral support—and lose them when you really begin to make your moves.

And if you can figure out a way to do that, please let us know.

MAKING THE PLAY:

KNOWING WHEN TO MAKE YOUR MOVE

" Eye contact is key. If you don't look at somebody, you obviously don't want to be around them." — *Chris, 18*

You've got all night to orbit, but only a finite number of chances to make direct contact with female life-forms. Why? Because if you indiscriminately start to hit on every girl in the room, word will spread fast; by girl five, you'll have mutated into a walking canister of Girl-B-Gone.

You must choose wisely, **approaching only** the women who have sent you some sort of telepathic go-ahead. But how can you be sure? Don't rush into anything. Take a moment to make sure you've interpreted her signal correctly. Consult the chart below for specifics.

"Don't try so hard. Women can tell when you're desperate. Don't chase them. Allow them to come to you. If you're that aggressive in public, how would you be in private?" *— Ronald, 24*

"As long as you address women with respect, they will address you in the same way." *— Aaron, 24*

SIGN	GREEN
She makes eye contact.	I swear she winked!
She does "the bathroom walk" (See "The Girl Gang," page 30 ♀).	I swear she brushed up against me!
She maneuvers closer to you at the bar.	She looked at my drink— maybe to see if I need a refill?
She sends you a note on a napkin.	She wants to meet me!
She seems to be waiting for you outside.	. . . in a red convertible with the engine running and passenger door open.

Watching the Signs

> **"**I don't believe in lines.**"** —*Chris*, 18

> **"**I just open with whatever is on my mind. Questions are good.**"** —*Carlos*, 21

Evolution of an Opening Line

Your eyes have met ... now how about the rest of you? At this point, all there is left to do is to bowl her over with a richly textured, lushly romantic, sparklingly witty humdinger of an opening line that she'll some-day embroider on a doily. **Right?**

YELLOW	RED
I could have sworn she looked at me, but now I can't find her.	Oh, *House of Style* is on the TV behind me.
I swear she gave me "the look."	Oh, I think her friend is sick.
I think she's trying to get away from my friend.	Oh, she's dating the bartender.
She wants to meet my friend.	Oh, it's a subpoena.
She's talking to the bouncer.	Oh, right, I'm the valet.

Wrong. If you come on like Joe Shakespeare, you'll come off like Joe Hallmark. When the cheese 'n' sleaze factor is too high, your line will trip her ultrasensitive BS alarm (which sounds a helluva lot like loud, mocking laughter). Read on to see how the crafting of an opening line can separate the smart guys from the wise guys.

LINE 1:

Uh, hi. I felt your phenomenal white-hot energy from across the room. You are like a human supernova. I could write a poem just about the way the light hits your hair. In fact, I have, right here on this napkin. But why don't I read it to you later over break-fast in my hot tub?

LINE 2:

Uh, hi. I saw you from across the room. You are, like, uh, really hot. You remind me of that song. Um, you know that one? Well, uh, anyway, do you wanna take off?

LINE 3:

Uh, hi. I know you. Aren't you the girl from the chip bowl? Yeah, we go way back. Man, it's hot in here. You wanna go somewhere and talk?

LINE 4:

Uh, hi. Hot enough for ya?

LINE 5:

Uh, hi.

"Original's good. But honesty is good, too." —*Lisa*, 21, on opening lines.

Listen up: Line 5 really works. Seriously. Sure, you've heard that be-yourself speech a million times. But if people really listened to it, it wouldn't be a speech that people hear a million times, now would it? Let the ladies think that you are so flus-tered and nervous by their power and beauty that "Uh, hi," is all you can possibly muster in their overwhelming presence. **They'll think it's cute, honest, sincere, etc.**

Or you can try the reverse strategy. We should pay homage to the hombres who can **dish out the smooth lines and get away with them** (or, more to the point,

go away with a phone number). If you want to be like these dudes, pay attention: This is the only time in this whole book when you'll be told to **skip the sincerity. Why?** Because no matter what, a line sounds like a line. But if you play your cards right, that can work in your favor. You can actually deliver a **lame-o prefab line,** but only if you say it with an ironic, inside-jokey tone of voice that says, "I know I'm slipping you a line. Work with me. It really can be effective." When it's obvious that you're joking, she'll laugh in your honor, not in your face.

Here are a few hackneyed openers that will work when used properly.

"What's your sign?"
(Never, ever do this one with a straight face.)

"Come here often?"
(Likewise.)

"Can I buy you a drink?"
(With today's prices, it's a sure bet, but it may be only because she's thirsty.)

"What's a nice girl like you doing in a place like this?"
(Best used in fancy digs—more irony.)

"This party's beat. Let's jump into my convertible and head out to the beach to watch the sunrise."
(Best if you reside in a landlocked state. And rode your bike.)

Opening Line Hall of Shame

1. Wow, are those real?

2. Nice sweater — sure would look good on my floor . . . or actually, on *your* floor — I live with my parents.

3. [In food-related situation] You're really puttin' it away, aren't you?

4. Are you on the Pill?

5. Are your legs tired? 'Cause they've been runnin' through my mind all night.

6. Are there mirrors on your jeans? 'Cause I can see myself in your pants.

7. You two gals wanna have a three-fer?

8. So, do you think I look like Leonard Nimoy?

What Part of "No Way" Didn't You Understand?

Sometimes even the **Sultan of Smooth** gets dinged. And sometimes even the Sultan of Smooth doesn't realize that he's getting dinged. If you're ever unsure, consult this **easy translation chart.**

IF SHE SAYS . . .	SHE MEANS . . .
That's sweet, but no thanks, I'm tired.	GO AWAY.
I'll be right back.	GO AWAY.
Oh, no, I don't feel well.	GO AWAY.
I'm waiting for my friends.	GO AWAY.
I'm waiting for my boyfriend.	GO AWAY NOW.
Oh, you're still here . . . ?	GO AWAY *NOW*.
I'm just getting over a relationship.	My last boyfriend dumped me hard. I still drive by his house three times a night and scrawl his name in lipstick on my mirror. Still want to dance? Don't leave me!

Battling the Bitch Goddess Small Talk

If the threat of dancing weren't bad enough, now you have the **bitch goddess Small Talk** to sacrifice yourself to. Even more complicated, you not only have to mind what you say — you also have to look, and you have to listen. Some guys, though, do know how to sweet-talk a woman. Take some advice from them.

SAY NOTHING STUPID

Your opening line may have gotten you this far, but **one slip of the tongue here and you'll get none later.** You'd think the safer option would be to say as little as possible, but give a **Mr. Monotone performance** and she'll get nervous and get the gift of gab that keeps on giving. At the other extreme, nobody likes **Phony Tony,** oozing cologne and schmoozing up a storm. Of course, you want to say enough to keep her from nodding off. When in doubt, use the shy-smile trick on her. She'll think it's kind of cute that you're a little tongue-tied.

And finally, if a real lollapalooza gets loose ("Actually, I think you look more like Charles than Di"), act natural. Move on to something else as if nothing happened. **Do not attempt to save your butt by (A)** pounding your head on the wall and saying, "Stupid! Stupid!" or **(B)** backpedaling ("Did I say 'Charles?' I meant 'Charo!'").

LISTEN TO HER, STUPID

THREE LEVELS:

BEGINNER: Nod attentively, knitting brow (if applicable, stroke beard thoughtfully).

INTERMEDIATE: Say, "Uh huh . . . wow . . . cool."

ADVANCED: Make appropriate comments ("Gee, I never thought about feminism that way before. But hearing you put it that way, I realize that sisterhood really is powerful").

WATCH FOR SIGNS

Here's the hard part: Concentrating on what she's chattering about and watching for signs. You **need an eagle eye.** There's a lot you can tell from what she does now about what she might do later.

HER BODY LANGUAGE	YOUR TRANSLATION
PLACES HAND BRIEFLY ON YOURS.	You're in! (unless she's removing it from her thigh).
OCCASIONAL HAIR FLIP.	This neck's available for nibbling.
HAIR FLIP WITH "ACCIDENTAL" LEG BUMP.	This neck and this thigh available for nibbling.
CONSTANT HAIR FLIP.	No go! She appears to be turning her head to summon help (See "The Girl Gang," page 30 ♀ .)
LOOKS AT HER NAILS.	Whoa! Easy, there! She's wondering how her hand will look with a big rock on her finger!
CROSSES HER LEGS, LEFT OVER RIGHT.	Whoo-hoo! She's giving you a chance to check out her firm step-class calves!
THEN CROSSES THEM THE OPPOSITE WAY.	Woo-hoo! Don't miss that *Basic Instinct* reference, buddy!
LOOKS AT HER WATCH.	How long do I have to wait before you come home with me, carry me up my ladder, and take me on my loft?
SPILLS WATER DOWN THE FRONT OF HER DRESS, LEANS FORWARD, AND WHISPERS, "OH, MY . . . I'M GOING TO HAVE TO SLIP OUT OF THESE WET CLOTHES AND INTO A DRY MARTINI."	Damn! She's a klutz! Can't take her anywhere. And you thought things were going so well.

IMPORTANT NOTE: When describing articles of female clothing in normal conversation, do not use any of the following terms: **panties, dungarees, slacks, blouse,** or **pocketbook.** Women hate those words.

GETTING THE
DIGITS

"If we are getting along well, just before I say goodbye, I usually ask, 'Can I call you sometime?' I just slip it in. Usually I get a yes." —*David, 24*

Gentlemen, getting her number should be cake. Some of us still don't realize how easy this can be. All you need to say is, "I had fun talking to you. Would you mind if I called you?" It's sincere, flattering, polite, direct.

Basically foolproof, unless she's married or unless the music drowns you out. You're in, you're out, you're on your way. End of story.

So why, why, why do we never say that?

It's REJECTION rearing its ugly mug again. When the **girl at the keg blew you off,** you took your business elsewhere. And when the **girl at the bar blew you off,** but then came and talked to you again before she left with someone else, you could deal. **You can take those kinds of party games, no sweat.**

But going for her digits gets you in way deeper. Say there's this honey you've been chatting up for a while, more than small talk, and the party's winding down. Now, if you dare ask for her number and she says no, that can mean only one thing: that **she actually does not want you to call her.**

Ouch!

Since getting her number is your moment of truth, time it carefully. Ask too soon and she may think you are looking for recruits for **Human Sacrifice Nite back at the Temple of Doom.** But wait too long and it might be *hasta la vista*, bonehead.

Employ this strategy: Pick up on something she says, and use it as your in ("Now that I see how powerful sisterhood is, I wonder if we could join forces in some way to make a real difference. I'm collecting names and numbers for Students for Change. Could I add you to our membership list?").

Once she reaches for pen and napkin, **be alert to those telltale signs that she's giving you a phony number.** You know, anything starting in 976 or 555. And **don't forget to check that area code.** A long distance number can mean either a lot of inconvenience (you know, all the driving back and forth) or a weight off your shoulders (the farther away she lives, the harder a time she'll have stalking you).

What to Say if She Says No

1. "Oh, that's okay, I got some things to take care of anyway."

2. "Oh, well, that's okay—see, my phone, it's no good."

3. "Your number? Oh, no, no, I said lumber. You see, I'm building my own chalet in the Alps for me and my fiancée."

4. "Well, hey, good luck to you."

5. "Well, you can't have mine, either. Nah-nah."

LOOKING AT LOVE THROUGH
BEER COLORED
GOGGLES

When you walked into that party, you said to yourself, **Tonight's the night.** I will spot a Claudia Schiffer look-alike, and she will be mine. **Oh, yes, she will be mine.**

But as the night wears on and the keg runs dry, your standards blur along with your vision (" Wait — I can't quite make her out—is she a **babe,** or is she **Babe?"**). Suddenly you're not so picky anymore. Hey, she's laughing at your jokes and she doesn't appear to be sending secret SOS signals (see "The Girl Gang," page 30 ♀). How wrong could you go?

Well, that depends. Be careful. One too many drinks—or one too many frustrating hours past midnight—can transform a swamp thing into a **sweet thing** . . . and back to a swamp thing when the rays of the morning sun dissolve last night's haze. Yep, last night she was Julia Roberts; this morning she's Julia Child. Last night, Linda Evangelista; this morning, Linda Blair. Sandra Bullock; Sandra Day O'Connor. **Get the picture?**

So have some fun, make some moves, and keep your mind open—but here's **what can happen when you let lust fog your lenses:**

BEER VISION

WARNING: Relative appearance of subjects in lenses varies with time and alcohol intake.

CHAPTER

3

HA HA HA

THE DATE

"Hi, I'm That Guy from the Party": Keeping Your Cool When You Make That Call. The Phone Call lifts that brush with beauty out of your softly lit party dreams and dumps her right into the cold, harsh light of reality. What if she doesn't remember you? What if her roommate answers and says, "Oh, hi, Paul . . . !" with a knowing snicker? *What if you get the machine?* (See page 46 ♂) Inside you, two primal urges are duking it out. In this corner, we have the urge to suck face. And in the other, the urge to save face. Sometimes the dread of getting dissed can KO even the loudest mating call. Get a hold of yourself. Be a man and pick up that phone.

FRIDAY

PARTY!

SATURDAY

TOO SOON
TOO DESPERATE

SUNDAY

TOO SOON
NOT DESPERATE
UNCOOL

MONDAY

TOO SOON
NOT DESPERATE
UNCOOL

TUESDAY

EARLIEST
POSSIBLE
CALL

NOW OR NEVER !!!

WEDNESDAY

THURSDAY

WEEKEND
COMING
UP!

FRIDAY

TOO LATE
FOR WEEKEND
PLANS
DON'T CALL!

SATURDAY

WAY TOO LATE
FOR WEEKEND
BRUNCH?
MAYBE?

SUNDAY

CHEESY!
TO CALL NOW LOOKS
LIKE YOU WERE
UNLUCKY OVER
WEEKEND

WEEK AFTER

CALL BY THE END OF THIS WEEK OR FORGET IT.

WEEK AFTER

ZONE OF TOTAL DESPERATION. SHE'LL THINK
YOU DUG AROUND IN YOUR DIRTY LAUNDRY
LOOKING FOR SOMEONE, ANYONE, TO CALL.

You can put your stress meltdown on ice by following these simple guidelines.

> " I don't think you have to wait. If you're interested, call her." —*Andrew, 21*

> " My limit is two calls, maximum. If I call a girl more than twice and she doesn't call me back, I just blow it off." —*Josh, 24*

A) WHEN DO YOU CALL? See opposite.

B) WHAT TIME DO YOU CALL?
Never call on the hour or half-hour—too planned. Attempt to call at times that end in three or seven, as in 9:33 or 2:37 (that's P.M.).

Talking the Talk

Before you dial, be prepared, or you'll risk inviting her to your great-aunt's funeral by mistake. **Try to split your phone call into the following phases.**

A) WARM-UP
Crucial. Label an index card **Lies I May Have Told.** If you said you were part of an elite antiterrorist Navy Seal strike force unit (hence the cast on your leg that prevented you from dancing), remember to get your story straight. **Now you are ready to dial, dude.**

B) IDENTIFY YOURSELF
Trickier than it sounds. Do not, repeat, do not stray from this simple formula:

First Name + Location of Meeting (as in "Hi, this is Keanu . . . from the bus?").

Stray from this boilerplate and you'll wind up in a mess of trouble. Here are two openers that just blow....

"Hey baby, guess who?"

"Hi, um, yeah, hi, this Keanu . . . um, I don't know if you remember me or not? But um, hi, I'm that guy you know, from the, like, the, um, bus?"

Let's get to the heart of the matter. You are calling for a reason, right? You don't have to waste precious seconds buttering her up or bending her ear with filler. **Cut to the chase.** If you wait too long, the issue of asking her out will just hang over your two heads like a big bloated piñata of pressure. It's hard to concentrate on what she's saying when you are trying to find just the right moment to slide in your invitation. **Once you get the question thing out of the way, you can always keep talking.**

What to Do if You Get Her Machine

1. **Hang up.**

2. **Redial.**

3. **Hang up again,** convinced she's screening her calls.

4. **Script concise greeting.** Read aloud (enunciate!). Time length to insure it does not exceed forty-five seconds.

5. **Redial.**

6. **Deliver greeting** that bears no resemblance to what you rehearsed.

7. **Hang up.**

8. **Damn!** Should you have given her your beeper number?

9. **Decide** that the die is cast; you will not call back.

10. Afraid to leave house, **phone for take-out.**

THE GAME PLAN

" In order to have a great first date, I try to find out what she likes to do. " — *Gary, 24*

" A nice first date would be a nice lunch on the beach, talking in the sunshine. If things go well, it could go into the evening. " — *Bruce, 24*

You can't just take a date back to your house to watch *Baywatch Nights* and eat potato sticks out of the can. The first date has to be special . . . but not too special. Take her to Chez Schmancy and she'll be tempted to get your ring finger sized—or, worse, she'll take the grand scale of the date as an attempt to conceal some other inadequacy.

▶▶▶▶▶▶▶▶▶▶▶▶▶▶▶▶

Here's a list of potential first-date venues and their essential qualities, as far as you're concerned. (See "Setting It Up," page 43 ♀).

DATE	GAB FACTOR?	SEE/ BE SEEN?
MOVIE AT THE MULTIPLEX	Nada. Unless you go for pizza afterward. And if you do, at least you'll have something to talk about. But if she talks throughout the movie, no pizza.	None, unless she's a trophy you want to show off to your buddy the usher. Good place for mercy date.
PLANET HOLLYWOOD	No pressure. Can't hear date over the blare of Coolio.	Yes, especially if your date is Demi Moore.
LAKERS GAME	She wouldn't dare.	Major. It's just you, your date, and about a billion other people. You might even wind up on TV.
HARBOR CRUISE	Big Time. If you're worried about filling dead air, catch a flick first.	Minimal—everyone is looking at their own dates or yakking over the railing.
LASERIUM (LIGHT SHOW, NOT TATTOO REMOVAL)	No pressure. Can't hear date over blare of Pink Floyd.	Minimal —everyone is either under fourteen or over forty.
IN-LINE SKATING	Easy. You can talk for hours about how much you suck.	A risk. You don't know how she looks in sunlight or spandex.

BUCKS?	HEARTS AND FLOWERS?	ACTION POTENTIAL? DO NOT DIS-TURB
Getting pricier, but a known quantity. At least you know she won't be ordering the most expensive item on the menu (but limit her trips to the snack bar).	Depends on what's playing. But if she's the type of gal who thinks *Die Hardest* is romantic, she's your queen.	Well, maybe if she's Alanis Morrisette.
Twenty dollars for a Baldwin Burger, but worth it if your date is Demi Moore.	Electric neon kills romance on contact.	Only in the event of power failure.
If the best you can do is obstructed view, spring for peanuts and stay home.	If you've got really good vibes and good connections, send her a love poem on the Jumbotron.	Whatever you can get away with in front of a billion people, we applaud you for.
Beaucoup. Unless the boat is named after her, or *Singled Out* is springing for it.	Can't go wrong as long as you're packing Dramamine.	Depends on size of ship, motion of ocean.
Check prices—cost may be included with admission to "Big Bang" show at Planetarium.	Only when "Wish You Were Here" comes on.	Place is oozing with raw adolescent hormones. Succumb.
Could add up, what with skates, safety pads, splint, etc.	Definitely. You two kids will look like you are in the love-theme sequence of this year's feel-good romantic comedy.	Only if you have time to shower first.

DATE	GAB FACTOR?	SEE/ BE SEEN?
GREEN DAY CONCERT	If you want, but bring throat lozenges.	Heaps. But don't let her stage dive.
EVENING AT THE IMPROV	No, or the comedians will rag on you.	Yes, but the comedians will rag on you.
WRESTLING CHAMPIONSHIP AT PALACE O' MUD	Ample opportunity for witty banter about the finer points of wrestler's technique.	Definitely the place to be seen.

YOU MAY WANT SOME PLAY, BUT LEAVE THE TOYS AT HOME

"Look nice, smell good, chew gum beforehand. Comb it!" — *RJ, 19*

"Personally, I like a man in a suit and sunglasses." — *Amber, 18*

We've already gone over the basic looks and their first impressions. She already knows your "type," and so far, it seems to have worked. Don't blow it now with distracting accessories.

ITEMS TO AVOID

DON'T WEAR . . .	UNLESS . . .
AN ALPHANUMERIC PAGER	You're a doctor
A CONSPICUOUS CELL PHONE	It's in your Saab
A WORK UNIFORM	You're a fighter pilot
GOLD CHAINS	You're the Sultan of Brunei
A NOSE RING	You're Ferdinand the Bull

BUCKS?	HEARTS AND FLOWERS?	ACTION POTENTIAL? DO NOT DIS-TURB
She pays for her own T-shirt.	Only if you have a backstage pass.	Could be—all eyes are on the stage.
Loads of stealth charges: Drink minimum, cover, therapy.	No way. The comedians will rag on you.	Yes, if you move to an out-of-the-way table to escape comedian.
Need extra cash for G-strings.	Yup. She'll feel like a queen next to the combatants.	No holds barred.

BLIND DATE
DECODER

A blind date, sports fans, is like kissing your sister. On one hand, it is a date; on the other, it's hard to get excited about. Could be that it's called blind because most of the time you wind up being led around by a dog?

So next time, you'll know better. When your friend (or more likely your aunt) calls up and says, **"Listen, my girlfriend's friend knows someone you've gotta meet,"** you've got to ask a few more questions— **and listen much more carefully to the answers.**

Then take what you find out and run it through this handy decoder—or risk another date with doom.

CODE WORD		MEANS
GREAT PERSONALITY		ugly
INTERESTING		ugly
SWEET		ugly
MODEL		for the "before" portion of Clearasil ad (ugly)
PRETTY FACE		ugly everything else
VERY SMART		very ugly
VERY TOGETHER		ugly and tired

But let's say, just in case, that you had no advance warning. There you are in the lobby of the Googolplex, wondering how you can possibly sit for two hours, even in the dark, next to Gargoyla, She Who Snorts When She Laughs and Sprays When She Talks. **Fear not, brave prince;** you have your gender on your side. A girl, in the same situation, would try to at least be "nice" and cook up some outrageous lie about why she needed to go now (see "Seeing Your Way through a Blind Date," page 48 ♀).

You, however, are a guy. Now, that does not give you license to be **out-and-out nasty,** but it does give you some leeway. If you know that you just can't get through that flick, meal, or cat show, just leave. Tell her you have to go, and leave. Don't give her a specific explanation, or she will try to help ("A relapse? Oooh, let me knit you something!"). **Just go.** She'll be mad at first, but eventually she'll blame your whole gender for the injustice, not you.

"On the perfect date, I'm always funny. Everything that comes out of my mouth is great." —*Derek, 24*

> **"** On our next date, he was kind of dull—just kind of going through the motions. I had to make all the conversation. **"** — *Lisa, 21*

> **"** The best date is just doing nothing, going nowhere. Just having a great conversation for four or five hours. **"** — *Mark, 21, Lisa's date*

All this buildup, and now, finally, you've got your butt on a real, live date (with a real, live girl—unless her name is RuPaul). Take a deep breath. You sought her out, wooed her, figured out what to wear, ran a comb through your hair, met as planned . . . and **now all you have to do is convince her to sleep with you.**

No, silly, there's more to it than that. You've got to convince her to **pay for dinner and *then* sleep with you.**

No, silly, that's not it, either. It's even harder than that. **All you've got to do now is *be yourself*.**

That's right, yourself. Not some line-spewin', gel-goobin', black-book-packin' smooth operator. Girls sniff out cheese dogs in a nanosecond. Sure, sure, you're not that bad. But sometimes it's easier to pretend you're some slickster than it is to stick your neck out and act natural. After all, if you are just being, like, normal, and she doesn't like you, well, then she just doesn't like *you.*

There is one tactic you can use to your advantage. Women think they are the only ones who have the dating scene sussed out, that we don't know that *phone call* and *dinner* actually mean *cover letter* and *interview* (see "The Calling Calendar," page 41 ♀). Don't let it get out, but there is such a thing as *masculine* wiles. The fact is, we are checking them out just as thoroughly as they are.

So now that you're sitting down to dinner with your chosen cutie, you need to watch her like a hawk. You know, for example, that if she requests two forks for one dessert item that she's already thinking puppies and picket fences.

Yikes. The trick is to do what men have been doing for centuries: Make her think you haven't got a clue. You know, fumble a bit with your napkin and toss in a few "ums" and "aw shuckses." **She'll think you're just another cute but clueless stud that she's got wrapped around her little finger.**

And once she thinks she's running the show, she'll reveal her true colors—and then you can decide whether or not they match yours. So sit back, relax, and make her think you're just another slab of tenderizable beefcake. While she's batting her eyelashes, here's what you're doing:

FIRST DATE INSTRUCTION MANUAL

Follow these guidelines and she won't know who's boss.
But you will.

> " I was kind of late, but he was really late. Like two-and-a-half hours late. The restaurant started to close and someone tried to set me up with the chef. When Mark finally showed up, he actually told the chef to 'stop hitting on my date.'" —*Lisa, 21*

> " I was late, and she was late. We really didn't have much dinner." —*Mark, 21*

Part 1: The Arrival

Here's the scoop. Be exactly ten minutes late. **No more, no less.** She thinks you're just another **typical *guy* guy,** unable to bring himself to ask for directions. **Sucker.** You'll

know exactly what you're doing when you get marked tardy. It's her first road test. And if she fails, it's back to the lot for her. When you pull up outside her door at 7:10:00 P.M., study her every move. Her reaction will tip you off as to how she'll perform over the long haul.

THE MOMMY DEAREST

Arms folded across chest, standing in open doorway. Look out. This is the kind of woman who'll shove her fist down your throat if she finds only lame carnations in her Valentine bouquet.

THE GOLDEN STATE WORRIER

She's inside, calling the state troopers. Look out. This is the kind of woman who'll worry that there's some sort of noxious pesticide on the carnations in her Valentine bouquet.

THE "WHATEVER" GIRL

Gracefully accepts apology, and moves on. No clinging vines in this arrangement.

THE INVISIBLE WOMAN

Hey, and it's 7:10 — where the heck is she? Give her ten more and be cool when she gets there. She may just be testing you.

Part 2: The Activity

Go figure. Women hate to eat in front of us, yet they insist on having dates in restaurants (see "Setting It Up," page 43 ♀). So yeah, you'll probably wind up in one of these places. Pay attention. Mealtime is real-deal time. **Once you hit dessert, you'll have all the information you need to decide whether this babe really gets your motor humming.**

Let's start with ordering:

| DIET COKE & RICE CAKE | I'LL HAVE WHAT HE'S HAVING | BUBBA'S BARBEQUE |

You can tell a lot just by how she orders her tuna melt pita supreme. If she says something like, "Ooh, um, is there cheese in that?" or "Can I have it on a rice cake? Oh, never mind. I'll just have parsley. And a Diet Coke.

With lemon. No ice," she's way too picky. And picky, son, is a red light. **Why?** Let's put it this way. Someone who nitpicks her way through a blue plate special won't burst into your boudoir with wild abandon. Then again, if she squeaks, "I'll have what he's having," you might want to order her baby back ribs with a side of spine. If, however, she goes for Bubba's Barbecue Jumbo plate with deep-fried pork rinds, you love this woman.

Then there's the meal itself:

WELL-MANNERED	BIB REQUIRED	ROBO DATE

Luckily, most girls come with manners. If she requires a bib with her cocktail, at least you can say you had drinks with Nell. But you usually don't have to worry about her talking with her mouth full. And contrary to popular belief, sometimes women aren't the chatterboxes they're supposed to be. If you need pliers and a welding torch to get robodate talking, deactivate the evening after dessert. When necessary, you can jump-start your honey by tossing out these handy questions, guaranteed to elicit more than a yes, no, or wow.

1. "Your hair. It's different from when I first met you. What did you do to it?"

BONUS: You win points for remarking on a noticeable change in her personal appearance.

EXCEPT THIS ONE: "Have you lost weight?"

2. "How hard is it to find a good pair of jeans?" (essay question).

3. "How could men improve their dancing?"

4. "How do you plan to balance the demands of career and family?"

5. "Brad Pitt: Why?"

Miracle!

Butt-Saving!

Conversational Techniques

Unfortunately, several of the most effective conversational topics can also be minefields: Step on one, and be prepared to plant that foot firmly in your mouth. Unless, of course, you've got these handy comebacks up your sleeve.

TOPIC	GOOF	RECOVERY
THE NAME GAME	"Yeah, I know Jodi. I hated her...	...for moving so far away."
TELEVISION	"Oh, yeah, that sucked...	...for all of us when it got canceled."
CURRENT EVENTS	"Princess Diana? What a freak...	...free country we live in, unencumbered by the slavish devotion to a declining, outdated monarchy that traps women in loveless marriages and futile power struggles."

Reaching for Your Wallet, or, Keeping Your Manhood Intact

"I like to pay for myself. It's the way my mom taught me." *—Leah, 18*

> **"I rarely let her pay. Unless it's my birthday or something. I guess I'm old-fashioned."** — R.J., 19

These days, who pays is not always a political decision: Sometimes, one of you will pick up the bill in order to avoid having to do math. It's the weekend, for God's sake. But otherwise, guys, times have changed. And that may mean that sometimes you're off the hook. **But just remember:** You can't have it both ways. Like, don't necessarily expect her to pay—and to give up her career to bear your child.

Even in this complicated world, there is one rule of thumb you can pretty much rely on when figuring out who should pick up the tab: **Who invited whom?** Why shouldn't she pay for your fajitas if she made the reservations at Guadalaharry's? Enjoy the fringe benefits of sexual equality.

Well, you should enjoy it, but unfortunately, the old double standard kicks in. She picks up the check and you still feel like a big wuss. So go dutch. Or at least gamble with an offer to pay for the whole thing, and when she refuses to let you, then settle for going dutch. (If you reach for your gold card, your date should at least make a token gesture toward the tab, or lodge a featherweight protest—"Oooh, at least let me leave the tip . . . !")

One final warning: Though splitting the bill can loosen the load on your wallet, it can be a burden in other ways. The word *dutch* to some women means whipping out a calculator, legal pad, and no. 2 pencil, and itemizing you down to your last cheese fry. **Stop her. Just pay.**

Part 3: The Aftermath

Eventually you are going to have to drop your date at her door. When you get to the stoop, the air will be heavy with musk and possibility—unless you've endured a total clunker of an evening.

When you're deciding between calling it a night and burning the midnight oil, trust your gut. Hopefully you've trained your gut to know that when she's fiddling with her napkin ring and staring at the choking poster she's already back at her apartment bitching about you to her roommate.

Sometimes you just know there's a big smacker waiting in the wings, no question, no matter what it may "mean" for later. Or you think she's sweet, but there's no more-than-friends chemistry—so maybe you give her a hug.

But if you make those plans based on *your* vibes alone, well, that's only half the battle. Because no matter how sure you are of your own feelings, you need to tread carefully where hers are concerned. Sure, she seemed into you over the Nacho Supreme, but **maybe she was just being nice.** Girls do that.

The signals she sends to you now are the most critical of the evening because, unfortunately, she hasn't been programmed to just come right out and say, **"Jeez, I'd really like to jump you,"** or even something as tame as, "Let's kiss but not make a big deal about it, because I'm really not ready to get into something heavy right now, **but I like you, and you like me, and as long as we're on the same wavelength, why not smooch?"**

Trust us. These words are not coming out of her mouth right now. Maybe later, but not now. Nooooo, that would be too helpful. You are going to have to make like Sherlock.

But sometimes you get signals so mixed that your head swims. Like when she hugs you and gives a nice little peck on the cheek. **What is up with that?** Obviously, she'll take the initiative, but is it a preemptive strike? It's not exactly a *Red Shoe Diaries* moment. But **if she really wanted you to kiss off permanently,** she wouldn't have given you any kiss at all.

Or what if she reapplies her lipstick just before the moment of truth? Does a fresh coat of **Do Me Red** on those pouty Drew Barrymores mean **"Kiss hard, man-thing!"?**—*or* is it a new layer of **Don't Muss Me, Pig-Dog** smacker sealant?

Or what if she invites you in, but **her roommates are all there in footie pajamas, eating Ben & Jerry's out of the bucket and watching *Thelma & Louise*?** Scary. You're one step closer to the inner sanctum—but are you about to be judged by a jury of her peers? What do you do? **These situations would mystify even Miss Manners.**

But make no mistake: Certain signals do come at you loud and clear—for example, if she gives you a firm handshake and says, "Thanks for your time; we'll be getting back to you," you have entered a nooky-free zone. And unfortunately, if you get this Clammy Wynette of a send-off: "Hey, a bunch of us should all go out sometime!" (See "The Wrap-up", page 56 ♀)—well, that rejection anvil has definitely creased your cranium. Next time (if there is a next time), she's bringing her own security detail.

Now what if she tries to plant one while you're plotting the quickest route back to your VW?

If you aren't crazy about her, you might need to **just come clean and tell the truth.** Like that you just had an incredibly painful emergency root canal done and your stitches will explode on contact with another person's gums. Naw, seriously, the best thing to do is to deflect by strategically turning your head and kissing her cheek (as if you thought that's what she wanted all along), then hightail it out of there before she can say *nightcap.*

Otherwise, if you think she's swell but aren't sure if the feeling is mutual, **take a gamble and pucker up.** After all, if she's already decided you're not her type, a preliminary peck won't make things much worse. **And for God's sake, don't maul her on the first go.** Making her gag probably won't make her night (See "The Puke," page 59 ♀).

So far we've been pretty negative, giving you tips on how to make the most of mediocrity. But **when you really, really like her—not lust after her, guys, but like her—** the rules change . . . or they almost go in reverse. If you think your future covers way more than a few hours of tussling in her waterbed, you want to take things slow. Real slow. Maybe even not kiss her. **You're treading lightly on the paper-thin eggshells of true love, young lad.** You want this one to be different, special. **Maybe holding off will make for even bigger fireworks later.** It's worth the gamble—**you don't want to screw up.**

Confused by all these contingency plans? Follow this flowchart.

THE DOORSTEP MOMENT OF TRUTH
WHERE DO YOU GO FROM HERE, AND WHY?

HOT! HOT! HOT!

You don't even care what you'll have to bail yourself out of tomorrow — this is about love in a vacuum, or an elevator, or wherever. Move to Wild Thang.

PICKET FENCES

You love her. *Love.* Like Rocky and Adrienne. Like Lancelot and Guinevere. Or whomever. Decision time: Either you love her so much that you must have her now, or you love her so much that you want to wait.

CHILLY RAY CYRUS

For whatever reason, you guys just won't be doing the two-step. Sure, you could stick around for the heck of it, but your best move is to get your achy-breaky butt back to the pickup. Admit it. This one's . . .

WILD THANG

This thing may not be going anywhere later, but — nudge, nudge, wink, wink — you're sure as hell not going anywhere right now. STAY.

More than lust. This goes deeper. If you can't help yourselves, well — dare we say — it could be the first lay of the rest of your life. STAY — FOREVER.

NOT A HAPPENING THING

The Domestic Thang is what's really going on. Hands off. Feels too sweet to sour with a cheap saliva swap. BAIL — FOR NOW.

Don't even bother. Dead air. Test pattern. Nobody home. C-SPAN. Kevin Costner. Get the picture? BAIL, BAIL, BAIL.

Wherever you end up—vacuum, elevator, etc.— The Doorstep Moment may reveal more truth than you think. Plan ahead, play it safe, and be sure you're packing latex.

So let's say the first date went off more or less without a hitch. You enjoyed the movie, found things to talk about over deep-dish pizza, even locked lips for more than a millisecond. Now the question is, was it a one-hit wonder—or is there enough material to head back into the studio? **You make the call. Or not.**

DOING A
DOUBLE
TAKE

> **"**The second time I saw her, she had cut her nails. I wasn't scared anymore.**"** —*Chris, 18*

If you're somewhere between ga-ga and gag-me about this gal, the second date can serve as the double check. Was she really cute, or were you just swept away in the excitement of actually getting off the Laz-E-Boy? Sometimes there's no way to tell without a repeat performance.

But no worries. Wise men decreed long ago that a second round of miniature golf does not equal a walk down the aisle. You are not, repeat not, "going out" or doing something equally dire, yet.

CHAPTER

4

If you like her, the trick is to let her know without making it sound too heavy. Sure, she loves attention, but like any self-respecting guy, **she freaks when she gets too much too soon.** Be cute but not scary. It would be "cute," for example, for you to read up on a few of her hobbies before your next date, but it would be "scary" for you to read her mail. In general, it's best to just wait a couple days and then **pick up the phone, bonehead.**

The worst thing that can happen is
you'll get dissed.

HOW TO TAKE A DUMP

Wait a minute. What do you mean, *dissed*? A stud like you? It can happen, and even the wimpiest dis can pack a punch. Who wouldn't be a little ticked? When she says "no thanks," what she's basically saying is she'd rather be with someone else—or even alone. Hard to believe.

So let's say you have a fun date, wait out the three-day call buffer, and get her on the phone.

YOU: Say, Lana, my friend just got promoted to fry cook and we're all going out for margaritas to celebrate—wanna tag along?

LANA: Oh, that's really sweet of you, Todd, but I think I'm gonna have to pass.

YOU: Okay, great, so I'll pick you up at eight.

WHATSHERNAME: Um, Todd? What I mean to say is that I don't think we should go on any more dates.

YOU: I'm sorry, what? Is that too late?

TROLL: Um, Todd? You're a really nice guy, but I'm afraid I'm just not interested in being more than friends.

YOU: Oh [pause]. Oh, yeah, that's cool, I mean, that's what I had in mind. I mean, it was just a bunch of friends, I mean, I didn't really think of it as a *date* date or anything. I mean, we're like, um, buds, right? So, I guess I'll see you around, right?

CUJO, DARK PRINCESS OF SALEM'S LOT: Sure, Todd. Whatever.

WHAT LESSONS CAN WE LEARN FROM THAT FATEFUL TRANSCRIPT?

1. Um, Todd? You're in **dis denial.** Happens to us all.

2. After you come to, be cool. **Don't grovel.**

3. Pick up the pieces, and **beat a hasty retreat.**

EPILOGUE

YOU (ON PHONE TO FRIEND): So, Tad, we on for margaritas?

TAD: Yeah, Todd. Eight. So, you bringing that Luna chick?

YOU: Her? No, man. I dumped her ass.

Um, Todd? Here's some information you might need for when you really do dump someone. In general, be gentle but firm. Women are usually pretty sharp, but you really don't want her to not get the hint (as in, "Well, maybe we can see a movie when you get paroled?"). On the other extreme, you don't want to be on the run from that pack of vengeful harpies she calls friends (see "The Girl Gang" page 30 ♀). Here are several approaches that you **can tailor to your individual dissing needs.**

" If you don't want to go out with someone again, be clear. She'll be far more insulted if you try to be all smushy. And *don't* sleep with her." —*Ronald, 24*

TYPE OF KISS-OFF	INTENTION
Reverse Psychology	To actively scare her off with second date invitation.
Elaborate Sitcom Lie	To cushion the blow by concocting a humongous fib that you and your friends have to go to madcap lengths to substantiate for the next three years.
No-Questions-Asked Lie	To cushion the blow by concocting a simple fib that hints at a humongous problem.
The Insanity Defense	Self-explanatory.
The Vanilla Ice	To dump her in such a wishy-washy way that your spinelessness repulses her. She won't call back.
The Waldo	To deal her out without having to deal.

Down, Boy!
Maintaining Your Studly Image

Here's the way it should work

DATE NO. 1 ▶ **PHONE CALL** ▶ **DATE NO. 2**

Unfortunately, it's not always that clean. Things get messy after your first trip to the omniplex because, after all, we have our pride. Neither one of you wants to look too eager, so consider the following.

"I'd like you by my side as I make my 100th visit to the flesh-eating insect exhibit at Sciencetown!"

"Well, you see, turns out I have to commute between here and Burkina Faso, because I'm the sole heir to the throne of the sheikdom of Drambuie. Oh, and I'm not allowed to date."

"I just haven't been able to feel much since the accident. It's not something I feel safe talking about."

"Hi, this is Todd. *Who are you talking to?* I was wondering if you wanted to go out this weekend. *Dammit, Todd, who is she?* Shhh! I'm trying to make plans! I'm sorry, Lana, that was Cybill Shepherd, one of the personalities that uses my body as a host. But she won't bother us anymore, darling."

"Hi, this is Todd. You're a really, really sweet girl. And I really, really like you. But it's just that I'm so confused about who I am and what I want. I think what I need to do now is work on loving myself."

"Hi, this is Todd. I'm not around to take your call right now. . . ."

1. DO NOT RETURN HER FIRST CALL

("Sorry, my roommate sucks with messages.")

2. POLITELY DECLINE HER FIRST INVITATION

("Sorry, poker night with Waterbuffalo Local 444.")

3. LET YOUR MACHINE PICK UP DURING A TIME YOU SAID YOU'D BE HOME (Um, you forgot.)

THE THIRD DATE: PUTTING HER TO THE TEST

Three strikes, and **she's out.** The first date was the **getting-to-know-you date,** and the second is the **"no, really" date.** On the first date, you might talk about Pauly Shore; on the second, you might talk about politics. On the first date, you may have ignored that little snort she makes when she laughs; if you noticed it on the second date, will you think it's cute — or annoying — by the **third?**

Before you head back for thirds, remember that this one is the **Big Kahuna** of **dates.** It doesn't matter where you go — a picnic under the interstate, a Stryper concert, or a taping of *The Price Is Right* — your job is to figure out whether you want to keep her or dump her.

This test should help. Take it as soon as you have a minute alone (and if you don't have a minute alone, you don't need us).

---

1. WHEN I'M WITH HER I FEEL:

A) **At ease**

B) **Conflicted**

C) **Her friend up**

---

2. SOME OF THE THINGS WE HAVE IN COMMON ARE:

A) **A love of the outdoors, fine wine, and country line dancing**

B) **Certain insecurities**

C) **Raw, oozing wounds from past relationships**

---

3. I CAN REALLY SEE US:

A) **Backpacking through Europe together**

B) **Playing phone tag for the next week**

C) **In court**

---

4. SHE REMINDS ME OF:

A) Elizabeth Hurley

B) Liz Phair

C) Queen Elizabeth

5. SHE'S DIFFERENT FROM ALL THE OTHER GIRLS BECAUSE:

A) She's not afraid to be herself

B) She went out with me

C) All the other girls have opposable thumbs

6. I LIKE IT WHEN SHE:

A) Nibbles on my neck

B) Gives me a monster hickey

C) Is denied phone privileges by the duty nurse

7. SHE MAKES ME WANT TO:

A) Sing

B) Shout

C) Move

8. SHE'S IMPORTANT TO ME BECAUSE:

A) I've never met anyone like her before

B) She's an opportunity to see if I'm ready to date again

C) My lab grade depends on her

If you answered *C* to more than three of the above questions, you need to dog-paddle back into the deep end of the dating pool. Life is too short for mercy dates. Put this ménage à deux out of its misery. But if your mademoiselle passes with flying colors, don't think you are out of the woods. Pretty soon you two are going to have to decide if you are hanging out — or *going out*.

THE BIG "R"?

THE POINT OF NO RETURN

"When I do date, I date. I spare no expense." —*Adam, 24*

Somewhere around the third date, you start getting into vocabulary trouble. Not vocabulary as in, she doesn't know the term *offsides*, but as in, you two puppies don't know what to call this thing you are doing. Heck, as far as you're concerned, you never need to call it anything. But let's face it, the question does come up.

When you first take somebody out bowling, it's not an issue. More than a few trips to Big Daddy's Pin Parlor, however, and you won't be able to dodge the "boyfriend bullet" much longer.

In the olden days, people actually used to "go steady." No ambiguity. Guy asked, "Wanna go steady?" Girl answered yes or no. End of story. No so-what's-our-deal wishy-washy business. You gave that coed your fraternity pin, or you didn't, and that was that.

In some ways, things are much better now.

It is possible to mess around with someone for weeks without ever having to discuss **"where you stand."** But more often than not, **free love has its payback.** If some women had their way, they would take you to a couples retreat to hash out your status after two dates.

	TERM
	COUPLE
	DATING
	GIRLFRIEND/BOYFRIEND
	GOING OUT
	JUST FRIENDS
	RELATIONSHIP
	SEEING EACH OTHER
	SEEING OTHER PEOPLE
	TOGETHER

LEGEND Number of handcuff symbols indicates estimated relative degree of freedom surrendered. The greater the number of symbols, the greater the threat to your stud status.

Relax. Sure, some of the words she throws around are scary. But it's not that she necessarily wants more from you, it's just that she has this need to give what you have **— whatever it is —** a name. **Humor her** (it's not like *we* don't have the urge to name certain special things in our lives). Use this phrase book to translate what she's saying.

DEFINITION

CAUTION. **Appear anywhere with her in broad daylight and this is what people will call you.**

Can be used only after one or two dates. Also, if she forces you to sit through a showing of all her photos and yearbooks from kindergarten to the present—and you go willingly—then you are dating.

Word that you pray she doesn't use, unless she's a guest on *Ricki Lake* (as in, "Girlfriend!"). This is the term that your mother will employ as soon as she finds out you have gone on one date.

Means she hasn't asked you to define the relationship yet. BONUS.

Depends on who says it. If you say it, you are calling the steps in this tango, as in, "Sure, we sleep together. But we are *just friends*." However, when she says it, it means, "No way am I going to sleep with you; we are *just friends*" (in which case your response should be, "What do you mean? I thought we had something going on!").

You hate this word, but chill. She uses it for everything. She has a *relationship* with her manicurist, for God's sake.

Either just starting to date or no longer a couple.

You are allowed to. She is not.

Sounds ball-and-chain heavy, but actually no big whup. Basically means you are prevented from making out with somebody else if you two are at a party *together*.

TREADING ON HER TURF

IMPORTANT: Your place is where you keep your stuff. Her place is where she lives.

You don't need to be told — though you may need to be reminded — **not to leave the seat up.** But there's way more to it than that. Whether you wind up over there for breakfast, lunch, and dinner — or just for **"a midnight snack"**— you've got to treat that place like your mother's house.

No, your grandmother's house.

Now, this lady may not even be the **Princess of Neatness.** That's not the point. She is the Lady of the House. And that means you're her loyal subject. So mind your *p*'s and *q*'s.

DO	DON'T
Take off your shoes when you come in.	Put them on the counter.
Take a shower in the morning.	Pee there.
Use a coaster.	Drink out of the carton.
Wipe up crumbs.	Wipe them under the covers.
Help with the dishes.	Put appliances in the dishwasher.
Take her clothes off.	Forget to fold them.
Put things exactly where she tells you to.	Ask why.

Meeting Her Roommates:
WORSE THAN MEETING HER PARENTS

Three things you need to know:

THEY KNOW EVERYTHING ABOUT YOU

As far as your buddies go, **you could invite them to your stag party and they'd say, "No way, man,**

you seeing someone?" Not so for hers. Let's say you made small talk in the cookie aisle with her when you met. **Guaranteed, within the hour, her housemates would be able to diagram your sentences.**

NEVER, EVER MAKE ANY OF HER ROOMMATES ANGRY

(except the one whom everyone else hates). **Remember, you are a guest in Girl Country. Their primary loyalty is to the tribe.** Annoy one of them and they'll all turn on you. Now, certain things you may be able to figure out yourself **(like don't molest the cat — she's a full-fledged member of the sisterhood).**

PRACTICE RANDOM ACTS OF MANLY KINDNESS

This does not mean that you should park your toolbox in the foyer and start spackling without permission (see above). But if they do need a lightbulb changed or a shelf installed, offer to help as a favor, not as Mr.-Know-It-All-Fix-It-All — **they'll rip out your lungs with their own Phillips-head screwdrivers if you do.** Just wash some dishes that weren't yours, bring kitty a catnip mouse—but don't go overboard. **They can sniff out a brownnoser from the driveway.**

GOING AWAY TOGETHER
WEEKEND GETAWAY OR BAD TRIP?

Some lucky guys wind up with women who understand the beauty of sitting still, basking in the warm glow of a twenty-four-inch screen — women who aren't always *planning things*. True, some women are mellower than others, but they all

have a Spastic Demon Camp Counselor lurking somewhere inside

packing lunch, organizing group excursions to scenic by ways and "important" art openings, and reminding you to wear a sweater and arrive on time ("Come on, we're meeting people!").

What this means is that sooner or later, depending on how in touch your honey is with her inner cruise director, she's going to plan a weekend getaway for just the two of you. Of course, she'll do all the planning. Sounds nice, right? But let's just get one thing straight. You might be going on a romantic getaway—or you might be going on a suicide mission. On one hand, this could be your chance to really get to know one another. On the other, when you get back, you may know way too much. So try and be good: If necessary, relegate yourself to the backseat, alongside that cooler she's packed with diet soda, granola bars, fruit roll-ups, and handywipes. Above all, you need to prepare your mental state as thoroughly as she's prepared your provisions. **Here's a guide to some of the potholes, pitfalls, and perks you may run into along the way.**

STOP NO. 1
ANCHORS AWEIGH
She will have offered to plan everything, from checking the oil to assembling enough supplies for a six-week trek across the Yukon. You love her for this. She is capable, thoughtful, together. Unfortunately, you soon find out that she also resents you for not pitching in.

STOP NO. 2
STEERING WHEEL OF MISFORTUNE
At first the top's down, the sun's shining, the tunes are blasting, and you're on the open road. But five miles out of town, the bickering begins. Get ready for gasps of panic if you are driving and pull within twenty feet of someone else's bumper.

STOP NO. 3
CUTE BED 'N' BREAKFAST (HER IDEA)
You would have been just fine back at Primitive Gulch Campground. **But noooo.** She's already booked you in The Louisa May Alcott suite at the Aunt Clara Fussybottom Olde Wayside Inn.

STOP NO. 4
DAYTIME ACTIVITIES
You want to visit the **Hacky Sack Hall of Fame.** She wants to barter for silver anklets with the local craftspeople. You stop speaking and go your separate ways.

Two hours later you meet back at the hotel: Museum was lame, craftspeople ripped her off. **You make up.**

STOP NO. 5

"BUT THE MAP SAYS THE FORTRESS OF SOLITUDE IS THIS WAY!"
While on a walking tour of the Pueblo de Guerras Estupidas, she launches a direct attack on your manly core by second-guessing your built-in, testosterone-calibrated compass. You stop speaking.

STOP NO. 6

BACK IN TOWN
So, are you speaking again? Or did she say at any point on the return trip, "Do you want to walk the rest of the way?" Let's look at it this way: Unless you have reservations at her place tonight, you might have to part ways at the border. If, on the other hand, you've kissed and made up (waiting for hours while she wrote all those postcards may have helped), congratulate yourself on making it through couple-customs. Someday you may even be able to book a long voyage on the *Love Boat*. If you can survive this, you can survive anything. Welcome back.

COPING WITH HER CLAN

For her, introducing you to the family is part of the routine. For you, it's more like a root canal. And no wonder: You can be fairly sure that Tipper and Al aren't going to let their darling Betty hang out with just anyone. You're going, you think, to have to undergo a battery of tests dealing with **your manners, résumé, lineage, tax returns, and knowledge of current events. And you probably will.**

But what you fear most is El Padre. Why? The mother will want to know if you treat Betty nice. The father will want to know if you treat Betty nice and can make a down payment on a mortgage. Therefore, **your first job is to win him over.** It's not as hard as it looks. Volunteer little autobiographical information, unless it can be used as an icebreaker that focuses attention on his teams, his job, or his garage (for example: "I used to drive one of those John Deeres myself. What do you think of the 154-KX?"). That'll get—and keep—him going. You may thus **escape your own interrogation.**

Once you've toured the yard, **your next job is La Madre.** Offer to set the table, and then use your powers of observation. Mom will offer you a glimpse of what your muffin will morph into in the future—the not-too-distant future at that. For example:

THE HOVERCRAFT. Asks you to set the table, then talks you through each place setting. Means: Betty will force you to help her pick out what to wear, then veto all your suggestions.

THE WALLFLOWER. Lets husband lead the conversation; spends most of the evening going back and forth from the kitchen to the dining room. Means: Betty is really loud.

DR. MOM WESTHEIMER. Sees no reason why you two shouldn't feel comfortable "sharing" intimate details about your, well, intimate details. Means: You have not slept with Betty.

MOD MOM. Sits on the floor Indian-style; discusses drug experimentation in the '60s, wild sex life with Betty's father. Means: Betty's voting Republican.

PARTY OF BETTYS. Betty's parents died in a car crash, leaving her and her four plucky siblings orphans. The scruffy eldest brother tends bar at the family restaurant while trying to look after his sisters and brothers, who nonetheless find themselves in a misadventure every Wednesday night. Means: Betty's very busy during sweeps.

Holiday Performance Anxiety

"Guys don't do anything polite anymore." —*Caroline, 18*

As if holidays **weren't stressful enough,** watch them fall only weeks into your "relationship" (or whatever you call it). **Just when several dates had gone smoothly,** she "happens" to let it "slip out" that there are only three shopping days left until her birthday. Excellent. You can't figure out what to buy for your mother, much less for someone whose middle name you don't even know.

Here's the dirt. From the day that chickadee hatched into girl world, she has been conditioned to give—and expect—recognition on all Special Days. And girls have a lot of special days. Her friends, for example, will give her colored pencils and stickers on the anniversary of the day she got her first bra. Now chill. You do not have to go to that level of detail. Nor do you have to do anything elaborate. In fact, that may make her nervous or unimpressed, especially if you purchase a massively extravagant gift that took you two seconds to pick out on the way to her house (for example, a mail-order Cheryl Tiegs Deluxe Mammoth Lots of Little Bottles of Smelly Stuff Bed & Bath Trunk).

However, not doing anything is not an option. She expects only a token gesture, but a gesture nonetheless. You can even get away with a deliberately amateurish handmade card. In fact, she'd be touched (unless you cut out and paste on letters from magazines and newspapers and deliver it to her door anonymously). **Here are a few additional gift guidelines.**

CLASS	CRASS
Take a picture together in an instant photo booth.	Send her an eight-by-ten-inch glossy of yourself.
Make her dinner . . .	. . . at Store 24.
Take her to a play.	Take her to see *Blood Sport: The Musical*.
Pick her wildflowers.	Ragweed is not a flower.
Give her a chocolate heart.	Give her a chocolate phallus.
Go on a long walk in the woods . . .	. . . after dark.
Buy her a bottle of wine.	Enclose a note about "popping her cork."
Get her a gift certificate . . .	. . . for Nightcrawler Depot.
Buy her a little plant . . .	. . . that eats insects.
Buy her a stuffed animal . . .	. . . from the taxidermist.

You may never know exactly what makes women tick, **but** you've learned a little bit more about some of their springs and gears. **You can handle** her parents **and** her roommates, her pets **and** her pet peeves.

Now, it's not that you necessarily want to ride off into the sunset with every woman you take to the Cheesecake Factory, but you do, occasionally, want to meet someone who is more than just a squalid one-night stand. That's why you put yourself through this whole sadistic dating ritual in the first place, bucko. When you go out trolling for girl creatures of the deep, there's always the

THE END?

chance that you'll hook the fierce babe of your dreams (or at least of this week's dreams). You know, one who can argue the finer points of the designated-hitter rule, and whip up a mean Mississippi Mud Pie besides. She's out there somewhere. But if you wake up on Monday chick-challenged, see page one, and take it from the top.